I AM JOHN

Saints and Sinners Book 1

Jez Taylor

Copyright © 2024 Jez Taylor

All rights reserved

The characters and events portrayed in this book are fictitious. Any similarity to real persons, living or dead, is coincidental and not intended by the author.

No part of this book may be reproduced, or stored in a retrieval system, or transmitted in any form or by any means, electronic, mechanical, photocopying, recording, or otherwise, without express written permission of the publisher.

ISBN: 9798321906286

Cover design by: Jez Taylor

Acknowledgement

As always I am grateful for the support of my wife, Sandra in helping me edit the book. Self-publishing is a challenging process and I seek your forgiveness if there are still typos or other small errors in the text.

Other books by Jez Taylor

Peter the Rock Series:
On this Rock
I Will Build My Church

I Don't care Who Started It.
(Semi-autobiographical fiction)

"If I want him to remain alive until I return, what is that to you?"

JOHN 21:22 (NIV)

PROLOGUE

The eastern edge of the Roman Empire: Circa AD30

The fish oozed oil, which spat and hissed as it hit the charcoal of the beach campfire. The smell of fish cooking filled the early morning air. The sun was just about up and its warmth was beginning to affect the day. It was springtime and soon the temperatures would rise and bring to life the full beauty of the land. The man watching the fish cook looked up and saw his friends hauling the fishing boat up the beach. One of them was running towards him. He was wet; he had jumped overboard and swum ashore. *Impetuous as ever* he thought. There was a plate of freshly cooked bread, some olives and cheese, and the fish, which was almost done. The man stood, stretching out his arms as a welcoming greeting to his friends.

"Welcome, my friends welcome. Bring me more of your fish to cook. There are many of us to feed. Come and have breakfast." His voice carried authority but at the same time was calming and gentle. His friends looked a little nervous as if they had not been expecting him.

As the friends ate their beach breakfast, the conversation became serious. The cook was in fact, their leader. They had thought him dead, but it appeared they had been mistaken.

"I will be leaving soon; follow my instructions. You will be in charge from now on." He pointed to one of the men sitting around the fire. The man nodded his assent. He had been forgiven for an earlier error of judgment. He quickly swallowed his mouthful of fish, wiped his hand across his beard and then down his robe to remove the oily residue of the fish.

"What about him?" He nodded in the direction of one of the others—the closest friend of the leader. The leader turned to look at the other man. Younger, his beard not so thick. He smiled at him; the smile was full of love. A deep love, the kind one friend has for another, 'I'll die for you' type of love.

"What of him? If I want him to remain alive until I return, what has that to do with you?" The words could have sounded angry and sharp, but they were spoken with love. He smiled again, picked up a piece of bread and used it to pick up a piece of hot fish. He blew on it, and then bit into it. Fish oil dribbled onto his beard. The subject was closed, and the conversation moved on.

ONE

Patmos AD 90

It was time to leave the island. He clearly understood that. The dream had been explicit. He sat up in his bed and expected the usual aches and pains to begin, letting him know he was old. They didn't, which was unusual. He sat there for a moment assessing his own body, mentally working his way around his physical self, testing each joint and muscle. When he went to bed last night he had felt his age, eighty-three. Today he was unsure, he felt about twenty years younger. Had he slept well? Were the remedies the local physician gave him actually working? He stood up, to make sure that he was not still dreaming. His legs felt strong, and the muscles in his arms appeared bigger. He crossed the room, opened the shutters and stared out to sea. The bright summer sun flooded the room and he shielded his eyes. In the far distance beyond the horizon, the mainland of Asia Minor and the port of Ephesus stood proud. He smiled as he remembered his life there. He had been on this island for years, exiled as an enemy of Rome. He had become accustomed to life's slow pace rather than Ephesus' hustle and bustle. He would be sad to leave but knew he was being called away. Perhaps this was why he was feeling so strong. He looked down at his body. It definitely felt and looked different. He stepped over to the polished copper mirror and looked at his reflection. He put his hand up to his face and felt it, moving his hand around his neck and chin. His beard was short and neatly trimmed and his hair short and not quite as grey as it had been. The loose skin that reminded him of a turkey seemed to have shrunk back into place.

"It is time," he said to no one. A smile crept across his face.

He began to gather up his belongings, such as they were and packed them into a small shoulder bag made of leather. On the rough wooden table were three scrolls, each sealed with wax. He would deliver them to his friends in Ephesus when he arrived. Looking around the small room for the final time, he closed the door behind him and headed off down the hill to the small port, the summer sunshine warming his body as he went. There was a spring in his step; the staff that he carried was no longer a walking aid; his eyes were sharp and bright, better than they had been in years. He was excited for the adventure to come.

Rome circa AD 300

"Johannes, we must leave Rome now. Emperor Diocletian and his general Galerius have ordered the arrest and execution of Christians as enemies of Rome. Soldiers are already rounding people up. We are in danger!" The young woman's voice was full of fear. She began scrabbling around for her belongings, finding things to pack into her leather bag. Her baby began to cry, sensing the anxiety in her mother's voice. She looked anxiously at Johannes who just sat in a chair with his eyes closed, seemingly unaware of the impending danger or the stress his young friend was experiencing. "Johannes, please!" Her voice was sharp. Johannes opened his eyes and smiled at her. Johannes was about sixty-five years old, Jewish by ethnicity, yet Christian in his faith. He was clean-cut, fit and remarkably strong.

"Lucia, you must not fret. The Lord has a plan for us I am sure. He will not abandon us into the hands of Satan, or anyone else, whether emperor or general. Have faith. Come sit with me for a while, comfort your child." Lucia dropped her bag and picked up her child. Johannes motioned for her to sit next to him. He made a fuss of the child, calming her down and at the same time calming Lucia as well.

"Lucia, you are my stepdaughter. I chose you after your husband was taken by illness. I swore to care for you as my own child.

Would I place you in danger?" As he spoke, a feeling of peace descended on Lucia, as it always did when Johannes spoke with her.

"Johannes, you are different to anyone I have ever met. You are wise and seem to know the scriptures so well. I suppose that is why you lead the church here. That is why people come from all over Europe to seek your counsel. You are renowned; famous for your wisdom and compassion. If you are arrested, your work will cease, and the Church will suffer. Is that what the Lord wants?" Lucia loved Johannes dearly as a daughter loves a father. She would not be able to bear it if any harm came to him.

Sensing her anxiety, Johannes stroked her hair to comfort her. She felt an energy transfer from him to her and her tension and worry left her.

"Thank you," she leaned in and kissed his forehead.

"I think it is time I retired to the country. The Church is strong enough here to manage without me. Let us go south and then make our way to Spain, where the influence of Diocletian is far less and the Church more accepted than here." As he spoke, he felt a surge of energy flow through his body once again. He smiled in recognition of what was about to happen.

TWO

Jerusalem circa AD 1099

The two knights dragged the old man through the streets of Jerusalem. He was semi-conscious after the torturous beating he had received at the hands of his captors. His face was bruised and bloody and his robe bloodstained. His beard was unkempt and matted with dirt. On entering the courtyard of the building where the commander of the armies of the Christian God under Pope Urban II had made his headquarters, the knights dropped their charge. He fell, hitting his head on the stone cobbles. He lay for a few moments, mentally assessing his physical state, checking each joint and bone. As far as he could tell, there were no broken bones.

"Get up scum!" He felt a boot kick him in the back, just hard enough to make him move.

"It is time to meet your fate. You traitor to the faith." The knight spat at him, the spittle struck home, hitting the old man on the cheek. A crowd began to gather; soldiers, pages and other servants waiting to see what would become of the old man, the traitor, the famous Johan—a legend in Jerusalem.

"This is Johan!" One of the knights picked him up by the scruff of his robe and dragged him to his feet. "This is the man, who collaborated with the Saracens, who betrayed his faith, who lived with the enemy and protected them from our righteous fight, and our God-given right to this holy city." Johan looked around the courtyard at the sneering faces, hating him because they did not understand the truth. They had been blinded by the lies of the Catholic Church. Suddenly he recognised where he was, and it brought back a memory from many years ago, many lifetimes ago. His friend had also stood trial here and had been beaten and led out to die.

"Speak, old man, defend yourself, why have you sought refuge in the company of Saracens, rather than in the bosom of your brothers in Christ?" Johan almost laughed aloud. *Brothers in Christ? If only they knew the truth.* His life was spent ministering to ordinary Muslims, turning them to faith in Jesus, and helping them escape the vicious clutches of the Sufis and Imams who used them for their own political ends.

Johan turned slowly, taking in the scene. The crowd in the courtyard impatiently waited for the swift execution of Johan the traitor. There was a rumble of thunder in the distance, dark clouds gathered, the wind pushing them towards the city. Spots of rain began to fall as the first rainclouds passed over the city.

Johan spoke with boldness, knowing that this would not be his last day on earth.

"I have indeed lived among the Saracens, but not as a traitor, but as a missionary, to bring them to faith in our Lord Jesus. I have not betrayed the faith, but honoured my Lord all my life. I am only being obedient to what it says in the Gospel of Matthew. *'Therefore go and make disciples of all nations, baptizing them in the name of the Father and of the Son and of the Holy Spirit, and teaching them to obey everything I have commanded you. And surely I am with you always, to the very end of the age.'* I am no more than an obedient servant of Jesus."

"Traitor!" One of the knights drew his sword and raised it high over his head ready to let it swing and decapitate Johan. "Death to the traitor!" As the sword was at its zenith, a flash of lightning struck the tip. The energy surged down the metal shaft, through the hilt and into the knight, killing him instantly. His body stood motionless for a second then the sword fell to the ground, clattering on the cobbles, followed quickly by the inert body of the knight. The smell of burnt flesh filled the air and smoke rose from the cadaver, his robes smouldering. The other knight fell to his knees. "Forgive me, Lord!" There was fear in his voice. The crowd began to cry out, wailing and screaming.

"God has passed judgment." "Johan is innocent!" Rain began to fall heavily, suddenly, as if to cleanse the ground. People ran for cover, away from the scene. The second knight remained motionless, arms outstretched to heaven calling on his God. Johan turned away from the crowd and began to walk out of the courtyard. There was an energy in him now, a new sense of purpose. *Time to go*, he thought.

London AD 1570

"Your Majesty," said the priest, bowing slightly as he spoke. "Please be cautious when you seek counsel from this man, John. He is not clergy, either Catholic or Protestant."

"Yet he knows the scriptures better than any of you." Elizabeth spoke with authority. She waved her hand around the room to indicate that she meant the gathered men in the room. She was in her council chamber at Hampton Court.

"We know little of his background. He is an itinerant preacher, living and working amongst the poorest people in London. He may be a threat to you." The priest was determined to get his Sovereign to see sense. He was also worried by the rumours he had heard about John the preacher. He did indeed know his scripture. There were stories of miracles, unproven of course, but nevertheless rumours. He seemed to be advocating some sort of religious freedom, living as Jesus would want us to live rather than following Church doctrine. In the mind of the priest, this was dangerous.

"Your Majesty, he advocates ignoring Church doctrine and following the Bible's teaching. This could lead to revolution." The priest's voice betrayed his concerns.

Elizabeth smiled at her priest, "You're scared, my old friend. He is not the first to advocate ignoring the church rules. That German, Martin Luther was doing that in my father's time. He interests me, I want to hear him. Bring him in." Elizabeth turned from the window where she had been looking out over the River Thames, watching the barges being unloaded; food and other provisions for the palace.

John bowed in the presence of the Queen. He had been around long enough to realise that he needed to follow cultural protocols. He waited, head bowed for the queen to speak.

"Arise, John, come closer, step forward." Elizabeth sat on a small throne in the council chamber. The room was full of her advisers, including her nervous priest. John took it all in. He had been in many places like this, over the years.

"I hear that you are advocating that people be free to live according to the Bible and not Church teachings. Is that correct, John the Preacher?" Elizabeth leant forward on the throne. She projected an air of power and authority that often intimidated ordinary people.

"Your Majesty, all I seek is for people to live as Jesus intended us to live, by faith in him rather than adherence to a set of rules designed to bind people and control them," John spoke with an equal sense of authority. Elizabeth was taken aback.

"You want people to be free? To choose which faith to follow, Catholic or Protestant?"

"With respect Your Majesty, neither Catholicism nor Protestantism is the answer in their current form. Faith in Jesus, his death and resurrection are all that matter." The priest stepped forward and began to speak.

"Is this not heresy, Ma'am? He is denying the Protestant faith and advocating Catholicism."

Elizabeth barked a reply. "I'll decide what heresy is. He has suggested no such thing. Be quiet!" She stared sternly at her priest, challenging him to respond. His courage failed and he shrank back into the line of advisers, many of whom were shuffling uncomfortably.

"My apologies, John, please continue. Enlighten me as to this new way of fulfilling our religious duty. I am keen to hear about a world where there are neither Catholics nor Protestants, just followers of Jesus our Lord. It sounds intriguing." She turned to her advisers, spread her hands out in an open gesture and said, "You have our full attention."

As John continued to speak to the queen, the priest whispered to one of his own personal guards who stood near him.

"As soon as he leaves the palace, follow him, arrest him and bring him to me. We will deal with this heretic swiftly and silently."

John left the palace and headed down towards the river, intending to hitch a ride back into London. It was a warm day and he felt at peace with himself. Elizabeth had listened to him. *Perhaps there is hope for the Church.* Something in his spirit told him to turn around. In the distance, he saw three palace guards emerging from the grounds of the magnificent Hampton Court Palace. They scanned the surrounding areas. John ducked behind a tree and kept out of sight. Something told him it was time to move on. He was no longer welcome here. He waited for the guards to move away and then headed off down the towpath away from London. As he walked, his old bones ached and creaked, but he knew it would not last. *What an adventure!*

THREE

Ypres 1915

The shells had not stopped raining down on the Allied trenches all day. The battle for Ypres was long and hard fought. The Allied forces had fallen back to within three miles of the town and dug in once again. Spring was turning to summer and the ground was finally drying out. The troops were weary, scared and hungry. Jan was a medic. He sat with a small group of soldiers in a ram-shackled bunker. They were his medical team. He was praying with them, trying to calm their nerves, allay their fears and comfort them in their grief. Grief and pain were everywhere. *How are humans still doing this to each other, even after all this time?* Jan looked at one of them, no more than a boy, Tom Brennan. He was crying and rocking back and forth. Jan stood, walked over to him placed his hand on his shoulder and began to pray. The words were unintelligible, but God heard and understood. A warmth spread through the young boy's body and he began to relax, peace engulfed him, his breathing settled and he calmed down.

"Listen!" said Jan quietly, pointing his finger up to the sky. "What do you hear?" The men huddled in the bunker fell silent and listened. "Nothing Captain, it is all quiet."

"Then it is time for us to get to work!" Jan began to issue orders to his small team of medics. Now was the time to collect the injured, retrieve the bodies, collect the identity tags, or dog tags, as they were known, from the bodies and begin to collate the data for the officers back at headquarters. As they emerged from the bunker with their orders, the men could clearly hear the groaning and crying coming from both their own trench and the strip of land between where they stood and the enemy trenches. No man's land.

Jan turned to the young boy whom he had prayed over and spoke gently to him. "Stick with me, don't wander off. Do as I say and you will survive." Tom nodded; a look of courage filled his face. Jan and Jan's God would look after him. They climbed the ladder, heaved themselves up and over the top of the trench; in a crouching run headed out into no man's land. For five long hours, Jan and Tom triaged the wounded and helped them back to the relative safety of the trench. They carried bodies on their shoulders, and scavenged body parts for the dog tags to ensure that families knew their young men had died with honour.

The sun was beginning to set, the cease-fire had held all day; Jan clambered over a mound into a crater followed by young Tom Brennan. There in front of them lay a wounded German soldier, his leg missing. He was dying. "Finish him off, filthy Hun!" Tom was tired and angry. Visions of bodies, blood and gore filled his head. Hatred for the enemy filled his heart. He stepped forward with malicious intent. Jan held up a hand to stop him. He knelt down beside the dying man and whispered to him in fluent German.

"Jesus liebt dich, mein Freund. Betet mit mir." The man's eyes opened. Fear filled him when he saw an enemy uniform but relaxed when he realised what Jan had said. Struggling for breath, he spoke. "Jesus ist der Herr." Jan began to weep, tears flowed from him.

"Mein Bruder, es tut mir leid. Geh zu deinem Herrn." Jan began to pray the Lord's Prayer in English, Tom suddenly realised he was reciting it too. The German soldier's eyes closed again and he took his final breath in the arms of Jan the medic. At that moment, a shell exploded about one hundred yards beyond them. The noise was deafening and the resulting debris began to scatter around them. Further shells followed, peppering the ground all around Jan and the boy soldier.

"Head down and follow me." Jan's voice seemed to give the young boy courage once again. Together they scrambled out of the crater and crawled back towards the English trenches. Shells fell around them, bullets fizzed above their heads, but with a grim determination, Jan led the young soldier back to safety.

"Cease fire!" The call was music to Tom's ears. "Incoming troops!" The officer's voice boomed louder than the big artillery guns. The shooting stopped; Jan could hear the shouts of his comrades urging them on. The young boy soldier scrambled down into the trench followed by Jan.

"You see, young Tom, follow me and you will be safe. Follow Jesus and you'll live forever." Jan held him at arm's length and smiled.

Tom Brennan sat in the damp and dark bunker, one candle his only light. He was writing to his fiancée back home in Sussex where he lived in the village of Findon. He wrote of the bravery and love of his Captain Jan, who had saved his life and shown a depth of compassion for his enemy that mirrored that of Jesus in the Gospels. He wrote that what he saw in his captain had convinced him that God was real and that he had become a Christian. He told of how Jan had disappeared shortly after; the rumours were that he had been transferred to another unit further along the trench. Tom never saw Jan again. After the war, Tom named his son John in memory of the man who saved his life.

FOUR

Germany 1942

The moonlight and the gentle spring breeze made the moon shadows dance on the forest floor, creating an eerie spectacle. Twenty scared people carefully made their way through the small forest pathways, led by an old man walking steadily using a long staff. He was in his early sixties with dark hair cut short and a neatly trimmed beard. He was strong and had an aura of authority surrounding him. The twenty scared people followed willingly, knowing he was leading them to safety.

"Hans, slow down, some of the children are struggling," whispered Jakob the leader of the twenty, who was a man of about forty-five. He carried a rucksack on his back, with all his worldly possessions packed neatly inside. Behind him was his wife, she led her three children. Beyond them, several other families all carrying small bags containing the last of their possessions.

Hans stopped, turned around, slipped his rifle off his shoulder and placed it against a tree. Hans knew the forest well; this was not the first group of Jewish families he had led out of the horror that was Nazi Germany.

"There is a clearing up ahead, we can rest there an hour, but we must be at the border before dawn." His voice was quiet but firm, commanding the situation. He pointed in the dark, along the path. The moon broke through and momentarily lit the way before darkness descended again. There were nods of assent and they pressed on towards the clearing and respite from the long march through the forests of Southern Germany.

Jakob sat against a tree trunk, one of his children asleep on his lap. His wife rested her head on his shoulder, trying to find peace and rest in this particular nightmare. He looked up at Hans, who had spent the hour patrolling the clearing, ensuring their safety, rifle on his shoulder and staff in his hand.

"You are a good man Hans. Thank you." In the moonlight, Hans saw him smile weakly.

"No, God alone is good, I am just his servant."

"Hans, you look Jewish but speak as a Christian. Who are you?" Jakob was intrigued by the compassion and wisdom of the old man Hans. Hans knelt before him and spoke quietly so as not to wake the others.

"I am Hans; I am of Jewish origin but I am also a disciple of Jesus. Come, we have no more time to discuss religion. What is more important is love. I must show my love for you by getting you to safety. Come on, arouse your friends, we must go."

An hour later, Hans and the twenty silently crossed a small river, wading up to their waists in the cold flowing water, the last of the snowmelt. Hans stood mid-stream, guiding them across to Switzerland and the safety of his brothers in the fight against Hitler. Later that day, in the safety of a mountain hostel five miles inside the Swiss border, Jakob wrote in his diary about the bravery of a Jewish-Christian called Hans who had rescued many Jews from the gas chambers by leading them through the forests of south-western Germany.

FIVE

Twenty-five years ago: Southwest London

The two fifteen-year-old boys raced down the high street dodging the shoppers. It was a busy Saturday three weeks before Christmas. It was gloomy and what sunlight there had been was fast disappearing as the afternoon rolled on.

"Last one to Maccy D's gets to pay!" shouted the blond scruffy-looking boy running ahead of the other. "That's not fair! You got a head start!" The other bellowed as loudly as he could. Just then a man who appeared to be about seventy stepped into his path. They collided and both went crashing to the ground.

"Shit! Aargh!" said the boy as he hit the floor, scraping his head on the pavement. The old man rolled over and sat up, apparently not hurt. "Woah! Steady on lad, you will hurt someone one day. What's the rush? The man sat up and shook his head. A crowd gathered around and tried to help him, but he shooed them away. "I'm okay, I'm fine. How's the lad? Is he okay?"

The blonde boy stopped in his tracks and jogged back to laugh at his friend. "Come on Sam, I'm hungry, get up. Look the old bloke is okay. Anyway look at this lot, they'll look after him." He turned and sprinted off to McDonald's. The old man had help getting to his feet, concerned shoppers stepping forward with Christmas spirit to help him. There were tuts and scowls aimed at the blonde boy and his disregard for compassion. Sam sat up and rubbed his head.

"Ouch, that bloody hurt!" he scrambled to his feet. The old man approached him and Sam looked anxiously at him. "I'm really sorry mate, I just didn't see you." Sam was genuinely concerned.

Onlookers began to bait him, telling him off for running, being a lout and a thug. Sam began to feel threatened and anxious. He was not really like that. In fact, he was more nerdy than anything else. The old man held out his hand. "No hard feelings." Sam shook his hand and a sense of relief flooded through him. The onlookers began to disperse, leaving the old man and Sam standing in the middle of the pavement.

"My name is Johnny," smiled the old man, "You are Sam, aren't you?" Sam looked surprised. "I heard your mate say your name before he rushed off." Sam nodded in understanding. Something about Johnny was different. It intrigued Sam. Most old people just shouted at you and told you to get your hair cut or stop misbehaving, but Johnny seemed different.

"How about I buy you and your mate a McDonald's and we can see if we can stop that cut on your head from bleeding. Sam touched his hairline and noticed a small dribble of blood.

"Why not, it's the least you can do after nearly killing me!" Sam held up a bloody finger and began to laugh out loud. Johnny joined in. "Come on son, my treat."

"What did you bring him for?" sneered the blonde boy when Sam and Johnny entered the restaurant.

"He said he'd buy us a McDonald's to say sorry." Sam was beaming and excited by the prospect.

"He's a bloody paedo, that's what he is. Buying you a meal? He'll be in your pants soon enough. You're scum, you dirty old man." His voice was filled with a deep-seated anger and hatred. He pushed past them and left. The restaurant had gone quiet as people stared at the scene that had just played out. Johnny could see the concern on Sam's face as he realised that this was indeed a strange man offering to buy him a meal.

"Sam, you're right to be worried, we've just met. I'm not a paedophile, a molester or anything sinister. I'm just an old man who lives in town. I help at the Salvation Army soup kitchen, go to the local Baptist Church, and clean at the local primary school. Now I couldn't do those things if I was paedo, could I?"

Sam nodded nervously. Just then, a woman of about forty stepped up; she wore a Salvation Army uniform. "Everything all right Johnny? Is this lad bothering you?"

"No, we're good. Aren't we?" He looked at Sam encouragingly. Sam nodded.

"Okay then, I'll see you at the soup kitchen tonight." She turned and left the restaurant carrying a brown takeaway bag.

Sam looked at Johnny carefully, sizing him up properly for the first time. Johnny was a fit and healthy man in his late sixties or early seventies. He did not have the look that normal old people have. He looked vibrant and almost glowed healthily. His skin showed his age but was not saggy or blotchy. He seemed to radiate vitality. His hair was greying and cut neat and short. He was clean-shaven. His eyes sparkled with life and he had a radiant smile. Sam began to relax. There was something about him he could trust.

"Don't mind my friend, Bobby, he hates all adults. Even his dad!" Sam spoke naively, not realising the trauma that his friend Bobby had experienced. Johnny nodded sagely and stepped forward in the queue to be served. They ate and drank at a table by the window chatting happily. Johnny had a way of making a person feel relaxed. Sam felt safe in his presence.

"Look Sam, no pressure, but why don't you and Bobby come to the youth group I help with at the Baptist Church; every Friday and Sunday? It's a lot of fun and you can meet some other teenagers too. We'd love you both to come."

"I'm not sure Bobby will come; he hates all religious stuff. But I'll give it a go. Why not? You've been kind to me when really I should have bought you a McDonald's."

Johnny laughed and ruffled Sam's hair. "Friday at 7.30 pm. Maybe

I'll see you there?"

Sam and Johnny became good friends. Johnny mentored him and guided him into adulthood. Sam ended up going to church until he left for university. When he returned, Johnny was gone. It seemed to others in the church that one minute he was there and the next, he had vanished.

SIX

It's not every day that your boss gives you a winning lottery ticket. To be fair, Sam Tucker's boss hadn't known it would be the winning ticket. He was trying to save money. The small chain of estate agents he owned was struggling and, as part of a much-reduced Christmas gift, he had given every staff member a Euro Millions lottery ticket. They had been received with a little less joy than the cheap bottle of Merlot bought from a discount supermarket. Sam was now a multi-millionaire. His winnings had been over one hundred million pounds, truly life-changing money. By way of a thank you, Sam had bought out his boss and then installed him as general manager over the chain. He invested in the business, updated it and it was now beginning to thrive. He and his wife Sally had done all the usual things that people do when they win the lottery: holidays, new cars, a new home and retirement from the rat race.

Sam had just turned forty-one. He was six-foot tall, and still quite fit, his Sunday football had kept him in shape. He had thick, dark brown hair, cut neatly around the sides but with a comma of hair that rested just above his right eye. His eyes were a piercing blue and he had a smile that melted people's anger. He looked out of his kitchen window across the fields. His newly renovated farmhouse was nestled in the South Downs National Park just north of Seaford, near the village of Alfriston in Sussex. The sun streamed through the window filling the kitchen with light. Dust motes danced and sunshine reflected off any shining surfaces. The sun was warm on his face and it made his body tingle. Just then, two arms slipped around his waist and squeezed him tightly. He turned his head and kissed his wife on the lips.

"Morning lovely! Sleep well?" Sally yawned in response. She was a couple of years younger than Sam and stood slightly shorter. Her hair was shoulder length, straight and was currently auburn. She had been blonde when they had first met, but she liked to colour it. Since he had known her, she had been, blonde, brunette, ginger, pink, green and even pitch black. Sam preferred her natural blonde but would never tell her so. Sally was slim, fit, pretty and, in Sam's eyes, way too good for him. She had been an accountant at a local firm and as such, shrewdly guided Sam to invest wisely, in both business and property. Consequently, their income was such that the remaining capital from their lottery win was rarely touched.

"I'm going for a run and then I'll have breakfast; I'll be about thirty minutes." Sally disengaged herself from her husband and left the room. Sam continued to stare out of the window. He was still getting used to living the life of a millionaire. It had been just over eighteen months since the win. He was standing in his farmhouse, looking out over the yard with barns, garages and other outbuildings. Four vehicles were parked in the yard. All his. Well, his and Sally's. A Range Rover, *well he was almost a farmer*. He smiled at his own humour. There was also an Audi A1 sports car, a Toyota Tundra truck and a Volkswagen T-Cross SUV. Sally had made him choose Hybrid or Electric vehicles where available and, at present, his Audi was plugged into a charging point outside the barn to the right of the yard.

He smiled at the thought of his wife. He always did. They had been together since they were at university. He had studied history and archaeology and Sally had studied something to do with maths and business. He could never remember the exact titles. It infuriated her. Every time it came up. Once again, he smiled at the thought. She was so sexy when she got cross with him. As he looked out of the window, enjoying the views of the rolling Sussex downs, two figures appeared, walking into the yard. The dog barked and scampered over to them jumping up to greet them. They saw Sam watching them. He waved and they responded in kind. Ian and Kelly lived in a cottage on Sam's land. He had renovated it and then advertised for a couple to manage his small estate. Ian and Kelly were well-qualified and were looking to escape London. They had quickly become good friends. Ian tended the large cottage garden they had developed; the plan was to open a 'farm shop' and sell local produce. The land would also sustain an orchard and even a small campsite. They had talked about glamping and creating a site with various tents, lodges and huts, all kitted out with the latest facilities. Kelly was creative and had already laid down plans for the site.

At that moment, Sally appeared in her running gear, stopped in the yard, hugged both Ian and Kelly and then jogged off. Sam sighed. *Thank you, God. I'm not sure what I've done to deserve this, but thank you.* He wasn't really a devout believer, but he had spent a few years going to a church youth group and had developed a passion for the Bible stories. More from a historical and archaeological viewpoint than a faith one. The thought reminded him of his task for today. He was writing a book about the Disciple John, a biography of his life and impact on the church. Since his lottery win, Sam had begun to indulge in his hobby of history and archaeology. He had already published a short book outlining historical myths and legends in England. He had been working on it for years. It was the success of this book that led a big London publisher to commission him to write a series of biographies of early Christian leaders. He rinsed his coffee cup under the tap and refilled it from the pot on the coffee machine. He opened the fridge and began to take out ingredients to make a cooked breakfast. It was Saturday, after all.

SEVEN

The Chairman sat at the head of the table, the agenda in front of him. He looked up and smiled. Around the table were half a dozen men and women, each with a copy of the agenda in front of them. The room was large, book-lined and musty. It reminded him of a Victorian mansion. Each time they met, it was in a different venue. This was his favourite so far. It gave gravitas to their work. He felt as if he were leading the cabinet like the Prime Minister.

"Shall we begin?" He smiled again. "Let's dispense with prayer." There was laughter from around the table. He said it every time they met, but each time it caused his colleagues to laugh.

"Item one. Secretary, I believe you are reporting on this." Each person around the table had a title. They never used personal names. A hood from a baggy black, sweatshirt shrouded each person's face. It was compulsory, partly tradition passed down the ages but also security was paramount and the less opportunity for detection by the public, the safer they would all be.

"Yes Chairman," the voice was female. "The attack on the synagogue was successful; the media believe it to be a Muslim extremist group that was responsible. There were no fatalities, unfortunately. That would have increased unrest and mistrust. All parties involved in the bombing have been paid in full. By that, I mean there are no loose ends." She finished speaking and sat back in her chair. There were murmurs of approval from the others seated around the table.

"Well done Secretary, I agree, the reports in the press show no indication other than a Muslim threat. My sources in government also suggest that they too believe this." He looked around the table from under his hood. "Item two. Treasurer, what have you to tell us?"

"Thank you Chairman, and may I congratulate the Secretary on an excellent job. I hope my report lives up to hers." He cleared his throat and continued from under the shadow of his hood.

"The fatal mugging of Christian activist, Simon Morgan, was accomplished with no witnesses. We have laid a false trail that will lead police to a local drug dealer whom Morgan was trying to 'convert.' It will look like he was involved in drugs and discredit his reputation as well. As always there are no loose ends." The treasurer sat back in his chair, and a smug feeling flowed in him. He had been successful. The Chairman would be pleased.

"Congratulations, Treasurer, Mr Morgan has been a thorn for some time; promoting ecumenism amongst the Church. A dangerous philosophy. If only the Church knew the power they possessed if they could only work together. I would say 'Thank God they don't' but I fear that would be hypocritical." Again, there was some laughter around the room. The Chairman continued. "We are The Six; New Atomists, we exist to destroy the infestation of religion in our land and indeed across the globe. All religion is false. It promotes unwarranted hope in divine beings that do not exist. All that does exist is the atoms that make us up and the space between them. Religion is a cancer that is limiting the freedom and pleasure we can have as atheists, scientists and hedonists. It is logical to destroy a cancer before it destroys us!" The last word was spoken with some force. The five others around the table applauded politely. This was not enough for the Chairman; he wanted to see a more public display of commitment. He stood. "The time has come, brothers and sisters for us here in the room to commit to each other in our duty. The six of us together. One mind, one passion, one goal." The Chairman lowered his hood to reveal his face. One by one each of the remaining five did the same, two more men and three women. The Chairman took in their faces. He, of course, knew them all from different walks of public life. They too knew him. He sat down and smiled.

"Administrator, tell us of your work in the Catholic Children's homes…" The meeting went on for a further hour, each team member recounting efforts to undermine the public face of religion in the United Kingdom. The sense of purpose and passion was palpable.

As the meeting of The Six drew to a close and the members dispersed, raising their hoods to hide their identity from any outside the room, the chairman spoke to the one remaining person. "Secretary, I am tense after the meeting, why don't you help me to relax." He rolled his shoulders to try and reduce the tension.

"Certainly Mr Chairman." With a swift movement, she removed the sweatshirt that covered her top half. Beneath, she wore a tee shirt with an image of the periodic table. She casually removed that too. She wore no bra. Standing in front of the Chairman, she unzipped her short denim skirt, and slipped it off, revealing brief white cotton underwear. She stood in front of the Chairman and smiled. He indicated she should sit on his lap. She obliged, and she straddled him on the chair.

EIGHT

Sam and Sally Tucker sat in the shade of a small restaurant in Rome near the Vatican City. The hustle and bustle of Vespers and taxis passed them by as they enjoyed their lunch. Sam sipped his cold Soave and looked up from his guidebook. His garlic and mushroom linguini had been delicious and he was feeling replete. He observed his wife. He smiled, he always did. She was people watching. It was her hobby: watching passers-by, wondering about their lives, and making up stories. He knew she would be doing it. She always did. Her plate was also empty. She turned from her observations of the people of Rome and picked up her cappuccino.

"What are you looking at?" She smiled as she spoke, knowing full well what Sam was about to say.

"You. People watching again? What's happening in the lives of these poor Romans?" He nodded at the passers-by. Sally stuck out her tongue and wrinkled her nose. Her eyes sparkled as she looked at her soul mate, Sam, the man she loved with all her heart.

"You can learn a lot from watching. Anyway, it's time to go; our appointment is at 2 p.m." She tapped her watch to emphasise the point. Sam closed his guidebook and finished his wine. Leaving a hundred Euros on the table, they stood and left the restaurant. Their waiter called after them.

"Same time tomorrow Signore Tucker?" His Italian accent changed some of the vowel sounds so it came out as, "Same a time a tomorrow eh Signore Tucker?"

"Maybe Gio, maybe." Sam waved at Gio as they left. They crossed the sunny street, narrowly avoiding a scooter being ridden by a nun, and headed up towards the Vatican City, holding hands, where they had an appointment with one of the Museum curators. It was early summer and the Italian sun was already hotter than the UK sun at its best. The cobbled streets were busy, they weaved between tourists and locals as the walls of the Vatican loomed large ahead. Sam was researching his book on John. The Vatican of course would have a great deal of documentation, some of which Sam was hoping to view.

"Signore Tucker, welcome. My Name is Father Luca, I am one of the curators here at the museum and archives. Luca was about sixty years old. He wore the traditional robes of a priest and a small black skullcap. His face was lined and leathery but his eyes sparkled with life. He walked with a slight stoop, perhaps from years of servitude and humility.

They shook hands. "Thank you, this is my wife Sally." Sam indicated his wife. She smiled and held out her hand. He took it and greeted her with a small bow. "Signora."

They followed Luca past the security checks and into a small modern office adjacent to the main Vatican library. Sam noticed the abundance of CCTV, monitoring every person. Once seated and coffee had been served Luca began with a question.

"Why John? What is your interest in him?"

Sam began to explain his interest in ancient history, particularly Biblical history, and the fact he had been commissioned to write about him. They chatted for about thirty minutes, Luca posing questions, eliciting from Sam exactly what he needed. Sally took notes on her iPad to ensure Sam had all he needed later on.

"In a moment I will show you to the archives where you can research further, under supervision of course. It is rare for a Catholic let alone a non-Catholic to be granted access. Your publisher must have great influence." He smiled a smile that indicated he didn't quite trust Sam and Sally Tucker.

"Of course! I am not sure how I got access. Connections in high places I assume. My publisher doesn't always tell me everything." Sam paused. "Do you have copies of the Acts of

John? Or later documents that suggest alternatives to his life after the resurrection?"

"What do you mean?" Luca was taken aback.

"Well, I'm curious about his grave and the stories that surround his old age."

"He is buried in Ephesus, go and see. What else is there to know?" Luca's tone had changed. He was suddenly defensive.

Sally decided to try and break the sudden tension. "I read a story once that John didn't die but was taken up to heaven. This was a popular tradition in the early Church." Sam carried the story on.

"Yes, in the gospel of John, the final chapter, Jesus says that John will stay alive until he returns. Doesn't he? So how can he be buried in Ephesus?" Sam was excited, this was just the kind of myth that he liked to explore.

"No, you are mistaken, the Gospel says 'IF'. Jesus does not say he will keep him alive. Visit Ephesus, see the grave, and put your mind at rest." Luca was agitated. "Come let me show you what we agreed." With that, he stood up and led them to the office door. The conversation was closed.

Sam and Sally spent several hours in the controlled environment of the archives. CCTV watched their every move, as did Luca. A host of ancient documents were stored carefully under strict environmental controls to prevent decay. Cotton gloves were worn to prevent damage to manuscripts. Monitors displayed electronic copies of many scripts to prevent over-handling. It was an historian and archaeologist's dream. Sam was in his hobby heaven. Sally too found it fascinating; she was slowly falling in love with Sam's hobby as well.

Sam leaned back from the reading desk where an ancient letter was spread out in front of him. It told of a man called Johannes who led the Roman Church in about AD 300. He was old for the time, wise, and kind. His knowledge of scripture was unparalleled. Sam looked at the letter intently but his eyes were tiring. The letter was written by a woman, Lucia his adopted daughter. Sam noted that in several places she referred to him as 'The Apostle' or the Lord's friend. *Curious.*

"I think we have enough, Luca, thank you." Sam put his iPad in his bag and Sally did the same.

"May we visit the library, as we are here?" Sally's eyes sparkled with enthusiasm. Luca turned and led them out of the archives leaving junior staff to replace the ancient documents in their sealed containers. As they walked up the old stone steps and out of the archive rooms, Sally whispered to Sam, "Did Luca get all defensive when you asked him if John was still alive? It seemed like he was hiding something. I wonder what?"

Sam leaned into her and quietly replied, "I expect it is because he believes or knows John to be alive!" Sally stopped in her tracks.

"Don't be absurd!" She had almost shouted the comment. It seemed to echo around the cavernous stone walls. Luca turned round in surprise.

"Signora? Is everything okay?" Sally nodded and blushed. Sam took a chance and stepped up to Luca the old priest.

"I just told my wife I think that you believe the apostle John to be alive." He let the words hang for a second and then continued. "She of course told me that was absurd!" Luca smiled nervously. Something in his eyes told Sam he was indeed hiding something. Luca laughed a little too enthusiastically as if to cover up something.

"Indeed it is absurd; The Apostle John has been dead for nearly two thousand years. He is buried in Ephesus. You must not waste your time on foolish fairy tales; they will only lead to disappointment. Come now let me show you the library." With that, he turned and walked at a pace towards the beautiful and famed Vatican Library.

NINE

The WiFi at the Palazzo Naiadi Hotel was working overtime in Sam and Sally's third-floor suite. They were in bed, both with their iPads scrolling through the internet looking for stories relating to the Apostle John, however absurd.

"Sam, you don't really believe the Apostle John is alive, do you? I mean that is ridiculous!" Sally pulled a face to indicate she really did think her husband had lost his mind.

"No, of course not, but Luca does, I'm sure of it. Now, what I want to know is why he does. What evidence is out there? It has to be more than just fairy tales and a line from the Bible." Every time they found something, Sam sent it to his server at home, where a specially designed piece of software would sort, catalogue, analyse the information, and then cross-reference it. It then created an intricate display of resources that could be accessed and read. Sam wished he were at home so he could look at all the information on his multi-screen display, but for now, his iPad would do.

Sally suddenly stiffened. "Sam look at this, I found it on an obscure historical legends website." She handed him the iPad and Sam began to read. It told of a 'divine' punishment meted out to a knight of the Crusades in 1099. Lightning had struck him dead just as he was about to execute a local man for giving charity to Saracens.

"Interesting, coincidence I expect, but that's all." Sam shrugged. He tried to pass the iPad back. "Look again, Sam, the man's name. Did you actually read the article?" Sam re-read the article.

"Johan!" He turned to Sally in surprise and then smiled. "Don't tell me you actually think…" He began to laugh, "Now who is being absurd?"

"No… but what if Luca knows this, maybe that's what convinces him? Stories from the past. Johannes from Rome, Johan from the Crusades… what if there are more? Perhaps he added these up and came to the conclusion John is alive!"

"Two stories don't make a case, Sally. There are hundreds of people called John in history."

Sally slumped back on the pillow. "Maybe you're right." She was deflated. Sam noticed and quickly moved to reassure her.

"Sorry Sal, I didn't mean to upset you. Look, I like the idea of this. It's fantastic. It's good fun. Let's keep looking, we can extend our trip; go to Ephesus, Patmos and Jerusalem if you like. If we find more stories perhaps we can incorporate them into the book." Sally perked up, recognising that Sam had made an effort to correct his dismissal of her find. She leaned into him and kissed him.

"I think I need to let you know that I accept your apology." She took Sam's iPad and placed both hers and his on the bedside table. She gripped her tee shirt and pulled it off over her head revealing her nakedness. Sam smiled like the Cheshire Cat. Sally snuggled in next to him and pulled the duvet over their heads.

As they made love and then slept, neither of them noticed the envelope that was slipped under the door of their suite. It slid across the marble floor and hit the ornate leg of the glass coffee table.

Sally tapped her phone and turned off the alarm. The sun was shining through the window of their suite. Sam stirred. Sally got up, walked naked across to the kitchenette area, and began to make coffee. Sam opened his eyes and watched his naked wife. He smiled, he always did. His body began to feel aroused by her again. He thought of the previous night and once again smiled.

"Come back to bed, we don't need to get up yet!" he was keen to get his hands on her again.

"Coffee is nearly done." She turned and carried two cups of coffee back towards the bed, her naked hips swinging gently. Sam couldn't help but grin at the sight of his wife. She was perfect in his eyes. She stopped halfway and looked down.

"What's this?" Placing the coffee on the table, she picked up the envelope. On the front, it had one name, Sam. "Looks like someone shoved a note through the door last night." She passed it across to her husband and went back for the coffee. Sam sat up in bed and opened the mysterious letter. Sally got in beside him and handed him a cup. He put it straight down on his night table.

"Look at this." He handed her the letter. It was a single sheet of Vatican notepaper with a handwritten note. Sally read it.

Take the 12.30 p.m. train to Latina today.

Take a taxi to Ristorante Giovanni on

Strada Lungomare.

Luca

"What? I don't understand. Where is Latina? Why does Luca want to see us?" Sally was genuinely confused. "This must be a joke!" She flicked the note away with some disdain.

"Don't you get it? We must have hit a nerve about something." There was a sparkle in Sam's eye. "Something he was not prepared to share in public at the Vatican. He wants to keep it a secret."

Sally wrinkled her nose. Sam loved it when she did it. She looked so cute and innocent.

"Really?" she said, "It's all a bit… Agatha Christie."

"What are our plans for today? Let's go for a trip to Latina, it sounds nice." Sam grinned. Sally shrugged. "Well, we had better get ready, then." She made a move to get out of bed but Sam caught her arm. "Not so fast, young lady!" He pulled her back towards him and wrapped his arms around her. "We have plenty of time." He pulled the duvet over them both and began to explore her body. She giggled at his use of 'young lady' but then began to moan as her body responded to his caresses.

TEN

It was another hot day, Rome Termini train station was busy; people with suitcases milling around, businessmen and women walking swiftly to make connections and families taking days out to Naples and beyond to the many national parks in Southern Italy. The Tannoy announced departures and arrivals.

Sam and Sally had no trouble looking like tourists on a day trip. Designer sunglasses and a backpack accompanied by tee shirts, shorts, sandals and straw hats. They bought tickets, headed off to the platform, and boarded the waiting train. The forty-minute journey south passed through the suburbs of Rome and out into the countryside skirting the small towns and villages before arriving at Latina station on the eastern edge of the town. As the scenery sped by, Sam and Sally chatted casually about Luca and the mysterious note. They were upbeat and enjoying an adventure that seemed to be from the pages of a mystery novel.

They paid the taxi and wandered into Ristorante Giovanni, finding a table in the shade just on the edge of the pavement. They sat down and ordered a bottle of a local house white wine. Sam soon discovered, after his lottery win, that paying more for wine did not always guarantee better quality. Local house wines were often better, being made in smaller, less industrial, quantities. A shadow crossed the table. They both looked up and saw Father Luca standing before them. He was 'out of uniform', wearing chinos and a cotton shirt.

"Luca, please sit down. You look so different out of the robes." Sam gestured for him to sit. He poured him a glass of wine, for which Luca was grateful. He sipped it nervously.

"Grazie. I waited not knowing if you would come. I am so glad you did." He scanned the street as if he were expecting to see someone.

"You look nervous, Luca. Are you all right?" Sally placed a hand on his arm. He turned and smiled.

"No one must know I am here. I have made excuses. My boss thinks I am visiting a sick relative in Firenze." Sally and Sam exchanged puzzled glances.

"Tell us Luca, why did you send us this secret note? It all seems very furtive." Sam held out the note. Luca leaned forward and spoke in a conspiratorial fashion.

"Listen. You seem like good people. I have researched you on Google and Facebook and all the rest. I need to trust you with something…"

"You hardly know us, Luca." Sally's voice was beginning to sound a little anxious. "What can you possibly trust us with? Why couldn't you just tell us in Rome when we met you?"

"Yes," said Sam, "Why all the cloak and dagger routine?" Luca looked puzzled. He did not understand the idiom.

"Mystery and secrecy," Sam clarified, seeing the look of puzzlement on Luca's face.

"Ah, I see. Let me tell you a story. Then you will understand my need for secrecy." He sipped his wine. Sally and Sam looked at each other in a way that indicated they thought Luca was one drink short of being drunk.

"Okay," said Sam smiling nervously, "fire away!" He took a big gulp of wine, topped up his and Sally's glass and settled back to listen.

"When I was a young priest in Milan, I came across an old man who spent his days distributing bread to the homeless. He occasionally would sit in my church and I would chat with him. He told me stories of his life, or should I say lives. At first, I thought he was just a forgetful, muddled old man trying to do a few good deeds before he died. But then I discovered a document in the archives in the Vatican when I was in Rome researching on Sabbatical. The document was a letter from a secret Catholic Priest, written to Pope Pious V at the time Queen Elizabeth 1st was excommunicated. It told of a rebellious preacher in London, advocating unity between the Catholics and Protestants. He met with Elizabeth and encouraged her in her move towards religious freedom. The priest had planned to secretly arrest him and execute him as a duty to the Catholic Church. However, the man vanished. The preacher was called John." He let the last word hang. Sally and Sam exchanged looks.

"I know what you are thinking," said Luca pre-empting Sally's response. "There are many Johns in history. However, my old man in Milan told me the exact same story, claiming he was that preacher John."

"Maybe your old man John had read about preacher John." Sam chipped in. Luca smiled knowingly.

"I challenge you to find any reference to preacher John in any history book, article or even novel. I have tried. There are none!"

"So what you are saying is that, on the basis of this one piece of evidence, you believe your old man in Milan to be the Apostle John?" Sally's interest was piqued.

"No. You made that leap. I did not mention the Apostle John. But since you have, and you clearly have an interest, otherwise why did you ask me about him in the archives, I will tell you that this is not the only story. There are many more that he told me. All of which I researched and found evidence of them being accurate." Luca stared intently at Sam.

"Why are you telling us this? Just because we asked about John? I'm writing a book; I don't believe he is alive!" Sam was both intrigued and frustrated by the story Luca told.

They ordered lunch of open sandwiches, salad and more wine, whilst Luca continued his tale.

"Years ago I told the then Archbishop in Milan I thought I had made a discovery that would enlighten the world and bring scientific proof of our faith. But I was told to keep it secret. I was inducted into a secret organisation in the Catholic Church working to verify all the myths and legends. To prove once and for all that God is real, Christianity is real, and to dispel atheism and other faiths forever." Sally nearly giggled, but Sam placed a controlling hand on hers. Luca missed the action, he was too engrossed in his story.

"Surely that organisation doesn't need to be secret. Wouldn't the Church want all the evidence they can get?" Sam probed.

"Agreed, but there are dark forces that are also at work here. Organisations that are working to undermine Christianity, Islam, in fact, all faiths." It was now Sam's turn to baulk at the ideas Luca presented.

"Don't tell me, the Illuminati!" Sam mocked.

"Humour me Sam. No, the Illuminati no longer exist. But growing from them are new, more powerful organisations that seek to control states, undermine faith and bring in an age of elite rule based on hedonism for the powerful and servitude for the rest. All these organisations are linked like the World Wide Web, controlled by a team of six in each region of the globe. Six is a key number. In religion, it is the earthly number, the number linked to Satan, whereas seven is the spiritual number linked with God. In your country, The Six is active and has already achieved a great deal in disrupting the reputation of faith communities." Luca paused as lunch arrived and the three of them began to eat.

Sam picked at his beef salad open sandwich with a fork, took a mouthful and then wanted to speak. Quickly swallowing his food, he asked.

"How do you know this? It all sounds a little far-fetched. What does it have to do with the character of John the Apostle? More importantly, what has it to do with us?"

"We're not religious, influential and we don't have anything to do with secret organisations." Sally, whilst interested in the story was becoming increasingly anxious.

"I'm getting to that." Luca topped up his wine. "Recently, I realised that our organisation has been infiltrated by The Six. As an archive curator, I can access all the documents and relics in the archive. Several have gone missing. All relating to 'sightings of John.' My work in trying to locate him has been compromised. My laptop was stolen, and my apartment was ransacked. I don't know who in the Church to trust. Any one of them could be working for The Six. My belief is they want to find John…"

"If he exists…" Sam interrupted.

"Sam!" Sally whispered sharply.

"It's okay," smiled Luca. "I know it is a lot to take in. If John exists, The Six plan to kill him, thus nullifying the word of God in the Bible and undermining the Gospel."

"So where do we fit in?" said Sam with a little sarcasm. Sally squeezed his arm to reprimand him. He flinched. "What do you want with us?" She asked Luca more respectfully.

Luca slipped his hand into his pocket and pulled out a flash drive. He slid it across to Sam.

"On here is all my research on John. The stories, articles, locations, and dates. Everything I have found in the last twenty years. I cannot carry on. I am being watched. That is why I denied everything quite clearly to you yesterday. I do not know whom to trust. If The Six get hold of this then they could find John and kill him. At the very least an innocent man called John may die if The Six believe him to be the Apostle."

Sally put a hand to her mouth in shock. "You really believe this to be true? They will kill?"

"Yes! But they do not know you exist. They do not know you are looking. You can find John and ensure his safety. You can keep him safe!" Luca sat back. His story completed.

For a few minutes they sat in silence, finishing their meal. Then Sam spoke.

"If I take the drive from you and follow up on your work, will it put Sally and me in danger?" There was concern in Sam's voice. "I mean; we're not detectives or professionals. I'm just researching a book."

"If you are careful and do not bring attention to what you are doing, then you are safe. It is only recently that I have felt I was being watched. You two can complete my research and keep 'John' alive. If he exists." Luca's tone was sombre.

Sam looked at his wife for reassurance. She nodded, but still with a look of concern and doubt. Sam reached forward and placed his hand over the flash drive picked it up and slipped it into his pocket.

"Thank you, and my God protect you," Luca's voice was filled with gravitas. He stood up and bowed slightly, "Arrivederci my friends." He turned and left the restaurant heading back towards the station.

"Have we done the right thing?" Sally was a little anxious.

"I don't know. But we need to get this uploaded to our server and the data analysed as quickly as we can. At least then, it will be safe. We can then plan what to do with it." He smiled, trying to reassure his wife. "What have we got to lose? I'm already researching the book, this may be helpful, and it may even lead us on an adventure in search of an immortal apostle. That's got to be fun, hasn't it?"

"I suppose so, It's all probably nonsense and in his imagination. He has probably saved you weeks of research, which means we can go and visit all of John's former haunts. It will be fun." She smiled and relaxed, having convinced herself her anxiety was all for nothing.

ELEVEN

The chairmen of the six regional sections of The Six faced each other on Zoom. Their hooded faces were unrecognisable to each other. The backgrounds blurred to provide further security. The European Chairman led the meeting. He was getting frustrated with the lack of support he was receiving from his American counterpart. On his screen, he could see the five other hooded figures, their regions identifying them: North America, South America, Australasia, Asia and the Middle East.

"I don't understand your position, North America. Why are you being so reticent? We have an opportunity to rid ourselves of an enemy." His accent betrayed his English origins.

"It is just that we still do not know what information we can gain from him. We have not recovered any data that may help us. For all we know he is just a priest. We do not need to kill him. Let us make sure we are acting in the best interests of the 'Six.'" His accent had a northern, New York twang.

"I agree, with North America," The voice was Chinese. "We must be cautious not to arouse too much suspicion. We have completed many successful missions in the last year and no one is suspecting a coordinated approach. None of the major government agencies across the globe has anything more than rumours. Why raise suspicion?"

"Kill him." The voice was from the Middle East Chairman. Her voice was typically Arab but her tone carried menace. "I have long advocated a much more aggressive approach. Why not attack the Vatican itself and destroy its archives? That would be a great victory for us!"

The European Chairman smiled, he could always rely on the Middle East to advocate violence. He wondered who she was and what she looked like. He began to imagine her naked and using her body for his own pleasure. He quickly had to refocus his mind. Those thoughts could wait.

"Thank you Middle East Chairman, your support is welcome. I too would welcome a large-scale attack. Perhaps we could talk in person one day about it and work together closely." If anyone could have seen the lecherous smile the Chairman had on his face they would have been disgusted.

"We need to vote; we have been here too long already. It is still possible that we can be monitored." The North American Chairman's voice was agitated. "All those in favour of killing the priest."

Emojis appeared in the chat, four thumbs up and two thumbs down. The European Chairman smiled. "Thank you, Chairmen; I will take the necessary action. We meet again next week." The screen emptied rapidly as the Chairmen logged off. The European Chairman sat in his office and smiled to himself. He picked up his mobile and tapped out a number. It was not in his contacts. "Secretary, we have a job to do."

TWELVE

"Look at this Sam," Sally motioned for him to come over. She was standing by an information sign that was written in English, Turkish, French and Japanese. They were in the ancient remains of Ephesus, specifically in the remains of the Basilica of St John. It was a blisteringly hot day and there was little shade. The area directly surrounding the tomb of John was roped off. There were several tourist groups, couples and individuals roaming the site. Ephesus itself was busy, it was the height of the tourist season. Sam and Sally had flown in from Rome to Ismir, hired an Audi from Eurocar and booked into a small boutique hotel in Selcuk a short drive from Ephesus.

Sam wandered over and peered over Sally's shoulder at the information sign. She read it aloud.

"This site was officially recognised as the tomb of St John in the 4th Century, and St Augustine stated that the earth above his tomb moved because the Apostle was breathing." Sally looked over her shoulder at her husband who raised his eyebrows and smiled. This was just what he loved. Exploring myths and legends. Sally continued, "Constantine had the tomb excavated but found no relics or remains adding strength to the legend that St John never died but was in fact taken up to heaven like Elijah and Enoch."

"We'll never find him, then, if he was taken up to heaven!" Sam was grinning.

"Stop it, Sam. It just means that even in the early church there were legends about him. And we both know that myth and legend have their roots in history."

Sam's phone pinged. He swiped the screen and a message appeared. "It's from Edna." Edna was the pet name he had given the software he had that searched, sifted and organized data on any topic it was given. "She's found another reference to John. He read out loud from his phone. "'Historian Tertullian wrote that John was plunged into boiling oil but remained unharmed.'" He gave a low whistle. "We also know that there is a legend that he was poisoned and bitten by a snake and escaped unharmed. This guy just won't die!" They wandered the site enjoying the scenery and the atmosphere. Sam taking photos for his book and making notes on his phone.

The main excavation of Ephesus was stunning. The wide pavements reflecting the sun off the white stone and the marble columns parading on each side made you feel as though you were back in Roman times. Sally snapped away with her Canon EOS R6 digital camera indulging in her own hobby. Sam was blown away by the amphitheatre where St Paul had nearly stood trial before the silversmiths and had eventually escaped a stoning with the support of the local city clerk. It was vast, and Sam tried to imagine the scenes he had read about as a teenager when he went to church in south London. There was something about all those Bible stories that intrigued him. *Too many coincidences*, he thought.

A child screamed. Sally turned around to see what was happening, as did many others in the amphitheatre. The sound reverberated around. *No wonder this was a theatre, it had natural amplification.* Sam was impressed. He looked at the scene playing out before him. A child had fallen over and tumbled down a few steps. His mother rushed toward him and scooped him up. Sally and other women in the vicinity ran to help, maternal instincts kicking in.

"Is he okay? Is he hurt? Look he has scraped his knee." Sally was first to the mother and keen to help. The woman nodded and forced a strained smile.

"Si, si. ...okay okay!" She backed away from Sally as the father arrived with the pushchair. He was a tall bulky man with a thick black beard. She too was tall but slender with her hair in a ponytail. They were dressed similarly to Sally and Sam, as tourists. The man stepped forward grabbed his wife's arm and pulled her away from the crowd that was forming around them.

"Hey," said Sally taken aback by the man's aggression. "There's no need for that." She held out her arm toward the woman to offer support. The man flicked it away as if it were a fly.

"Ow! Ouch that bloody hurt! What the he..." Sally was in pain, her arm throbbed.

"Hang on mate, that's my wife. You can't just..." Sam grabbed the man's arm to turn him around, but he was shaken off. Undeterred Sam tried again. He grabbed the man's arm and spoke forcefully.

"I said, you can't go around hitting women like that! That's my wife. You apologise..." The man a good few inches taller than Sam and clearly stronger turned around, rage on his face. He stepped close to Sam and grabbed his shirt. Before Sam could react, the man shoved him back and Sam fell against some steps, lost his footing and tumbled over. Sally shrieked!

"Sam!" She rushed over and bent down. "Are you okay? Did you see what..."

"I'm okay, only my pride is hurt." He let out a deep breath and shook his head to clear his thoughts. When they both stood up the crowd around them parted. There was noise and chatter, tourists gathering to see what the fuss was. Some filming and others posting on social media. The man, the woman and the child were nowhere to be seen; lost in the throng of the summer crowd.

"What was that about? I only went to help the woman with her kid." Sally was indignant.

"Some people don't like to be helped. Forget it. Put it down to experience." Sam was sore from falling over but he wasn't going to let Sally know. "Come on, let's get back to the hotel. I need a beer and a bath."

THIRTEEN

They bathed together in the large roll-top bath, easing away the aches and stress that the day had brought. The small boutique hotel was well furnished in a traditional Turkish style, the rugs on the floor looked antique and expensive. They spent an unexpected forty minutes in the king-size bed before heading out to a local restaurant where they ordered a mezze platter for two with vine leaves, hummus, baba ganoush, and an array of crudités, yoghurt and cheese. They followed that with Tavuk Sis which was chicken cubes served with bulgur wheat, onion salad, grilled tomato, and green pepper, accompanied with yoghurt and pide bread. Sam chose a local white wine to accompany the meal. As they ate and drank, the unpleasantness of their visit to Ephesus faded away. They spoke of the stories of John, the legends and potential theories to explain them. They both found the mystery more intriguing. It was drawing them in, seducing them, drilling into their minds until they were both almost convinced that the Apostle John was still alive. That the words of Jesus had come true.

"You realise what this means Sal, don't you?" Sam sipped his wine and topped his wife's from the carafe. "If we accept that John is alive, that the words that Christ spoke recorded in John's Gospel are true, it means that pretty much everything else about Jesus is true as well!" He set down his glass and stared across at his wife. He smiled, he always did.

"I hadn't thought about that. But you are right. If John is alive, then it does mean that all the things that Jesus said about himself and taught were and are true. That's life-changing." She held out her hand across the small dining table and took Sam's. She squeezed it. He responded. "My God, I am not sure I am ready for this. This is too big. I've always been sceptical of organised religion. Too many fakes and too many money grabbers." Sally's eyes betrayed her confusion.

"Me too," said Sam, trying to reassure her. "I've always been agnostic and ambivalent, even when I was a teenager and going to the church youth club. I was really only there for the girls." Sally wrinkled her nose and narrowed her eyes in a mock show of displeasure. He began to think back to his teenage years in Southwest London. "Thinking about it, my youth leader was called Johnny, he must have been in his seventies but looked really fit and healthy. Maybe he was the Apostle John?" He laughed as he spoke but somewhere in the recess of his mind, he wondered, *what if...*

"That would really be too much of a coincidence, don't you think? I know loads of people called John, they can't all be the apostle. Let's focus on what Edna throws up. Investigate that first and then move on from there. See if we can find any patterns."

"Yeah, you're right. It's just that Johnny was so kind, knew the Bible inside out and then by the time I got back from uni, he had vanished. No one in the church knew where he was. He had just disappeared. It's just weird, that's all." He finished his wine and topped it up again. They ordered Turkish coffee and prepared to spend a couple of hours in their room following up on the leads that Edna, their software programme had given them.

FOURTEEN

The following morning, they drove down to the small port of Kusadasi and boarded the weekly ferry to Samos. It was a hot summer in the Aegean and the sea breeze from the ferry was a welcome relief. They sat on the deck enjoying the journey. The ferry was busy, full of backpackers, holidaying families and locals commuting to and from various islands.

They had booked a quiet hotel just north of the town of Samos. The benefit of being a multi-millionaire was that you could always find somewhere to stay, even at the last minute. They had three days to wait before the ferry to Patmos, the island where John the Apostle had been exiled.

"I think we need to make a serious plan of action. To check out every piece of evidence and find any patterns that might lead us to John." Sally was enthusiastic.

"I agree, but we also need to take it slow. Remember what Luca said. The Six don't know we exist, if we rush about following clues about John then we might raise suspicion. Let's do touristy things for two days, enjoy Samos and work on the plan at night, in bed. That way we won't arouse suspicion." Sam smiled smugly at his own plan.

Sally leaned over and whispered in Sam's ear. "I'd quite like to arouse something in you, especially if we're in bed." She sat back quickly as Sam turned to her. She winked mischievously.

"Mrs Tucker, how dirty of you. But an excellent idea! I think I'm going to enjoy Samos." At that moment a woman carrying a child walked past them, she was pointing at a passing ship, talking to her child, her back to Sally and Sam. Something made Sally look up. For a moment, she thought she recognised the woman.

"Hey, isn't that the woman from Ephesus?" She nudged Sam. He looked up but the woman was gone from sight engulfed by a crowd of backpackers.

"Where? I can't see her?" Sam sat up and tried to peer through the crowd.

"I'm sure it was. Well, maybe. I can't be certain." She relaxed. "Perhaps that incident yesterday affected me more than I thought?" She shrugged and leaned back on the bench on which they sat. Sam put his arm around her and kissed her on the head.

"Maybe. It's unlikely we would bump into them again. It would be a massive coincidence."

Samos was beautiful. They drove around the island stopping at quaint villages and eating lunch in tiny restaurants. They spent an afternoon on the Mare Deus beach swimming in the Aegean and drinking cocktails from the beach bar. At night they ate in the hotel and spent the evenings on their balcony planning further trips to locations where Edna had discovered evidence of the Apostle John. At night they made love and slept in each other's arms. They played the role of rich tourists perfectly, because that is, in fact, what they were.

Patmos was much smaller than Samos and they booked into an exclusive villa near Petra Beach. It had its own maid/cook. They planned to stay a full three days to explore and attempt to locate any evidence of John's existence on the island. Sam was sure there would be plenty of legends and myths. They would return to Ismir via ferry, rid themselves of the hire car and then catch a flight back to Athens and then on to Tel Aviv.

They drove inland from their villa up into the mountains to the small town of **Choraon**, at the heart of which was the Monastery of St John the Theologian. The scenery was stunning. The higher they climbed into the hills, the more stunning the view of the Aegean Sea. The monastery itself blew them away. Set on top of a prominent peak it was more like a castle with whitewashed houses creating the town below. They parked in one of the small town squares and began to wander the winding streets, shaded by olive and cypress trees. The whitewashed houses and cobbled streets created a tranquil atmosphere despite there being many tourists. They found a café that had seats in the shade under a sycamore tree and ordered beer. From where they sat, Sally could look down on the square below them, where more cafés, bars and shops were crowded with tourists. She began to engage in her hobby of people-watching. Sam got out his phone and began scanning through Edna's messages, hoping for more leads on John. Suddenly he froze, and the colour drained from his face.

"Sal, look at this." He held out his phone. It was a news article from an Italian paper. She scanned the article, took a sharp intake of breath and put her hand over her mouth.

"Oh, my God!" She looked at Sam. "I can't believe it. We were just talking to him a few days ago." Father Luca had been found dead, having been missing for two days. He had been tortured, beaten, and shot twice in the chest and then in the head. His lodgings, inside the Vatican, had been ransacked.

"Police are at a loss to explain why he would have been a target. They think it was a Mafia hit because of the style of execution." Sam was scanning the rest of the article.

"You think it was The Six?" Sally looked anxious. "What if it was and what if he told them about us?" She grabbed Sam's hand. She was scared. "What if they come for us?"

Sam tried to sound reassuring but he was just as unsettled as Sally. "They won't, they don't know who or where we are. The whole point was that Luca wanted us to carry on. Why would he tell them?"

"Yes, but they killed him!"

"We don't know that, it could be unrelated. It could be a coincidence." Sam wasn't convinced even though he was the one saying it.

They debated and discussed what to do next. Both of them were anxious but at the same time, they both had a desire to solve the mystery of John the Apostle.

"I feel a kind of loyalty to Luca like we should fulfil his wishes. He obviously trusted us." Sally looked at her husband nervously.

"I agree, Sal, but at the same time, we're not detectives or secret agents. I'm an estate agent and you're an accountant. I want to solve this puzzle just like you do. But not if it costs us our lives." Sam held Sally's hands and squeezed them tight. "I love you, Sal. I promised to protect you and cherish you when we got married. I didn't promise to let you get killed by some mysterious organization that wants to wipe out God."

Sally smiled, leaned across the table where they sat and kissed him. "Stop being so dramatic. I have no desire to get killed. We have an advantage. They don't know we exist, and we're tourists, you're writing a book on John anyway, so you have every right to be going to places where he went. We have the perfect cover." She smiled again. "I'll admit I am shaken by Luca's death. It adds a serious side to his tale and makes me think there is some truth in what he said. Shouldn't we stand up for truth and justice? Isn't that what good people do? Luca said we were good people. We are, aren't we?" She looked at her husband with a look that always made his heart melt. He sighed.

"Okay, but at the first sign of danger, we stop. We tell the police and let them take over." Sally nodded and smiled, but inside, her stomach tightened. Had she just signed their death warrants?

Sally watched the tourists in the square below, backpackers, families and several photographers carrying tripods and large bags loaded with equipment. Patmos was a photographer's dream. Suddenly the colour drained from her face and she almost yelped. She held out her hand and grabbed Sam's arm. With her other hand, she pointed. Sam followed the direction of her arm and gaze. There below was a family. A tall, slender woman with dark hair, a small child in a pushchair and a tall broad-shouldered man with a bushy beard.

"No way!" Sam hissed. Sally looked at him, fear in her eyes. He patted her arm. "They're just tourists island hopping like us."

"But we're not, are we? We are just pretending. What if they are too?"

Sam thought of one of the lines from one of his favourite books. *Goldfinger,* by Ian Fleming.

"Once is happenstance, twice is coincidence, the third time it's enemy action."

"Okay, let's see if it is a coincidence or enemy action?" Sam stood up dropped a bill on the table and headed out of the café. Sally hastily gathered up her bag and followed.

"What do you mean, 'enemy action'?"

"It's a line from a James Bond book." Sam quoted the line and then continued. "Let's make ourselves visible to them and then see if they pop up wherever we go today. If they do, then we'll change our plans and disappear for a while. Throw them off the trail."

"You sound like a bloody secret agent. 'Throw them off the trail!'" Sally grinned. "You're enjoying this. You've changed your tune. What happened to not wanting to get me killed?" Sam smiled. "The Bond girl always survives." *Well nearly always.* He thought of the final scene in Fleming's *OHMSS* where Bond's new wife gets shot in the head as they drove off into the sunset. His stomach tightened.

They sauntered down to the square where they had seen the family and did their best to be visible. They wandered in and out of shops and bought a few gifts for Ian and Kelly back home on the estate. It wasn't long before they saw the family. They almost bumped into them coming out of a small church. To Sam, it was clear that they had been recognised. There was shock on the man's face. He quickly ushered his family away.

"Enemy in action?" said Sally.

"Definitely!" He took Sally's hand and they casually walked behind the family until they caught up with them. As they overtook them in the narrow cobbled street, Sam spoke.

"Let's go up to the monastery now. I'm sure we can get some good shots for my book."

"Yes, and after that to the Cave of the Apocalypse. Apparently, that's where John wrote the book of Revelation." They play-acted it perfectly. Chatting like no one was listening. Two tourists deciding where to go.

FIFTEEN

The Monastery of St John the Theologian was even more impressive close-up. The 11th-century structure was full of arches, passages courtyards and a wall-top walkway. The Church inside was bold. From the marble floor to the gold-painted Iconostasis and the vaulted ceilings painted with scriptural scenes, it was breathtaking. Sam and Sally followed a tour party around. Sam asked several questions that would help with his book. Sally snapped away, casually checking for the presence of their shadow family. Once the tour was finished they wandered the walls and found a quiet, shady place to sit. A monk walked along the parapet toward them. Sam called out to him.

"Padre, may I speak with you? Do you speak English?"

"Aye, I do" Sam was taken aback. His accent was Geordie. "Before ye ask. Am takin' a sabbatical from Iona in Scotland, where I am based. I am researching John and the Book of Revelation. Trying to see his inspiration, beyond God, that is!" He smiled as he spoke.

Sam held out his hand "Sam Tucker, this is my wife Sally."

"Father Patrick. Catholic and proud. I am a proper Catholic; I actually believe it all." They shook hands and a short-term friendship began, just for the time they would speak. Sam explained who he was and his research for his book on John.

"What do you think of John? Do you think he died? Was he taken up to heaven or is he still alive like scripture suggests?"

"Howay man, that's a lot to take in." Father Patrick sat down on the parapet. "Well, the people of Patmos all think he is alive. Well, the devout Catholics do anyway. There's a strong tradition here that after he wrote Revelation he just disappeared, but the scrolls turned up in Ephesus." He rubbed his chin as if it helped him think. "Look, I've been interested in John all me adult life.

I na all the stories. I've heard all the rumours. But faith is faith. It don't rely on concrete evidence. I don't care if John is alive or dead, man. It makes no difference to the truth of Jesus. That's what I believe."

"But surely, if he is alive," said Sam, "that would prove your faith."

"Aye, it would. But then there'd be no faith. You'd have no choice, no freedom not to believe. That's not God's way." Sam turned away to check on Sally. She was busy photographing everything and anything.

"Look, Sam. Don't go getting obsessed with the trivial. It only leads to disappointment and frustration. Keep your eye on the main thing. I'll tell you one thing though. Go to the Taverna St Maria in the bay, where the island narrows in the south. Speak to Maria. She'll help you further." With that, Patrick stood and held out his hand. Sam took it. They shook hands. He waved politely at Sally who was some distance away and then wandered off.

"Well that was surreal," he said to no one. Sally approached him grinning. She held up her camera to him to show him some pictures. One, in particular, she was very pleased with. Sam looked closely. It showed a family. Husband wife and child in a pushchair.

"They're here," said Sally with a mixture of excitement and trepidation. "Let's head off to the Cave of the Apocalypse and see if they follow. Then we will know for sure."

"That monk was very interesting," said Sam, as they walked down towards the exit of the monastery, passing another tour just beginning. "He gave me some good information and another lead to follow. Fancy a meal out tonight?"

They drove the short distance up the winding mountain roads to the Cave of the Apocalypse. It was much smaller and less impressive than the monastery but still, once inside there was a sense of history, power and spirituality that reminded Sam that there may be bigger forces at work in the world than just humans. They stopped in a small taverna for lunch and sat on an outside table in the shade. They ordered vine leaves, hummus pitta bread and a small carafe of local wine. They sat, ate and waited.

It wasn't long before the family arrived in a black SUV rental. The mother fussed about getting the child into the pushchair whilst the bulky bearded husband stood around watching the vicinity, taking in everything. Searching. His eyes locked on Sam and Sally. Sam was tempted to wave but decided instead to ignore him. It was better to feign ignorance than give themselves away. The bulky man turned away casually, but not casually enough. Both Sam and Sally saw the hesitance in his movement, the stiltedness. He had made a mistake and been clearly spotted.

"What shall we do?" Sally whispered, a glass of wine at her lips to cover her speech.

"Nothing. Let's finish our lunch, saunter back to the car and ensure that the Hulk over there knows where we are going. If they turn up there, then we confront them." Sam picked up his wine and took a big swallow, sat back in the chair and relaxed, knowing the trap was set.

SIXTEEN

Maria's Taverna was beginning to get busy with the evening tourist trade. The bay was no more than a few fishing boats, a small jetty and some large sheds. Around it were scattered isolated properties and homes, but right on the beach was a taverna. This was Maria's. Sam and Sally sat at a table on the terrace sipping a local red wine. It was rich and fruity and left a sweet taste on their palate. They picked at their food nervously, waiting for the Hulk and his wife to arrive. They had been clear enough about their intentions earlier in the day, deliberately speaking loudly within earshot of their enemy.

"What if they don't show? What if they do show?" Sally was nervous, either way.

"They will. When they do, we will confront them. If they don't, then we were wrong all along." He smiled at Sally. "Come on, it's fine. Remember, this was your idea, Sal." He held her hand across the table.

The waiter approached, followed by a tall, slender woman carrying a child and a large hulk of a man with a big beard. He showed them to the table next to where they sat. Sam and Sally stared at one another in disbelief. Sam raised his glass.

"Here we go!" There was a twinkle in his eye.

For a few minutes, there was an awkwardness between the tables. The Hulk and his wife ordered food and drink and then sat in silence, the woman feeding her toddler olives and feta cheese that the waiter had placed on the table. Sam took a deep breath and turned to the hulk-like man.

"Excuse me, but it seems to me that you have been following us, ever since we saw you in Ephesus. We saw you on the ferry to Samos and then again, here on Patmos. Wherever we go you go! Can you explain that?" Sam tried to keep his voice calm but the more he spoke the more aggressive he became. "My wife and I are just on holiday, I am also researching a book. So why are you following us?" The hulk turned towards Sam, there was frustration on his face. His wife looked concerned.

"I don't know what you are talking about, I too am on holiday. It is just a coincidence." He spoke English with a thick Greek accent. "Now leave me alone."

Sally broke into the conversation unable to hold back. "No, we need to know who sent you. Are you here to kill us?"

"Sal!" Sam barked. Sally shrunk back a look of shock on her face. Sam never shouted at her.

Sam stared at the man. "Well, is she right? I was trying to be more subtle, but my wife has a point." The Hulk's wife held out her hand and touched her husband's arm. There was a look of resignation on her face. Her husband understood the look. He moved his right hand to the inside left of his sports jacket. Sam jumped up out of his seat and moved to protect Sally. Instantly, the Hulk withdrew his hand.

"It's okay, it's not a gun. It's my phone. I need to show you something. If you want, you can get it from my pocket." He held open the left-hand side of his jacket. Sam looked at his wife nervously. She nodded. He reached across and took out a mobile from the man's jacket. The Hulk held out his hand and Sam handed it over. Sam's heart was racing, the adrenaline was pumping, and his breathing was shallow. He sat back down and noticed his wife had a tear in her eye. She too was trembling. He squeezed her hand whilst the Hulk searched his phone.

"Look, watch this." He slid his phone across the table. Sam picked it up. He pressed play and a recording began to play. It was Father Luca standing with the Hulk and his wife and child. He began to speak.

"Sam, Sally. If you are watching this, then you have met Christos and Maria. You can trust them with your lives. They are my closest friends. I made this film straight after we met in the restaurant. Ask them what you ate, and they will tell you. They can tell you everything we said and spoke about. I asked them to protect you. To work with you. Please trust them." The clip continued and Luca further endorsed Christos and Maria. Once it finished, Sam sat back and took a deep breath and Sally closed her eyes and began to cry quietly, the emotion taking over. Sam pushed the phone back to Christos. There was silence for a moment that was broken by the waiter bringing drinks and food.

"Why were you so aggressive in Ephesus? You really shook us up!" Sally had recovered and was almost angry as she recalled the occasion.

Christos spread his hands wide in an open gesture. "Let us get introductions over with and then we will explain everything." He paused to see if there was agreement. His beard separated to reveal a big grin. Sam smiled and held out his hand.

"Sam Tucker and this is my wife Sally." They shook hands.

"I am Christos Megalos, this is my wife Maria and our son Thomas." He beamed with pride. Everyone greeted each other and Sally blew a kiss at Thomas who giggled.

"How old is he? He is such a sweetie!" Sally took a risk. "May I cuddle him?"

Maria spoke swiftly in Greek to her son, who then held out his arms for a cuddle. Sally scooped him up.

"He is nearly three years old. He is a good boy." Maria's English was more stilted but easily understood. Sally held the boy close and kissed his forehead. "What did you say to him?" she asked.

"I told him you were an aunt and Sam was an uncle, part of the family, and that he was to love you both as such." Sally was taken aback.

Christos began to speak. "Let me clarify a few things for you. To help you understand." For several minutes Christos outlined his longstanding friendship with Luca, their shared interest in John the Apostle, their work to find him, his understanding of The Six and the dangers they posed. Sam and Sally asked questions, checking and double-checking, trying to test the validity of Christos and Maria. At every turn, they found only integrity and reliability.

"I was in the Greek army for many years and then worked for the Greek security services. I retired when I married Maria. The life of a spy is not for a married man." Christos picked up his boy and kissed him. "Other priorities come along. Undercover surveillance becomes a challenge with a child. I was cross at myself for allowing us to get too close to you. My apologies for the aggressive approach in Ephesus. Maria chastised me severely for that." Again he grinned. As the evening progressed they all relaxed and spent time getting to know each other, building trust. They ate and drank until late, Thomas asleep in his mother's arms.

Christos leaned forward. "My contacts in the services around the world tell me The Six is high on their agenda. They know of their existence and structure but cannot yet identify who they are. They live in the shadows. Those we have caught, the lowlife, refuse to speak. They are fearful. Some have even died in custody. It seems The Six are everywhere."

"And Luca?" Sam was unsure if Christos knew about Luca's death.

Christos and Maria looked at each other and reached for each other's hands. There was a deep sadness in their eyes. "We have mourned our friend, and vowed to find his killers and exact revenge." There was a hardness in Christos' voice.

"Were The Six responsible?" Sally spoke quietly, leaning into the table.

"Yes, they had been monitoring him. They believe John to be alive. They want him dead to undermine the truth of the Christian faith. They thought Luca knew where John was and was protecting him. That's why he chose you to give all his data to. You have the perfect cover to go looking. In Luca's data, you will find John, I am certain of it. We must protect him."

"But if John is alive and has been for two thousand years..." Sam felt ridiculous as he spoke. *How could anyone live that long?* "...then he doesn't need anyone protecting him!"

"True, my new friend, but it is also about protecting the secret. If the public knew of John's existence, then every old man would be in danger. Fanatics, terrorists, and believers would all want a piece of him. Many lives would be at risk. Innocent blood would be shed. It could bring chaos to the Western world and its belief systems."

Maria, shuffled position to make herself comfortable, trying not to wake her son.

"The Six need to know if John is real and alive. When they have proof, they will make it public. It will destroy confidence in Islam, Judaism, Hinduism and all the others. If they show Christianity to be true, it will most certainly cause religious wars, increase persecution and begin to destroy the peaceful coexistence of faith in many parts of the world. Then if they kill him publicly, faith in Jesus goes as well. The word of God failed and atheism will rule. That is dangerous because atheism cares only for the individual, survival of the fittest. It has a hedonistic approach to life where the strong do as they please and the rest suffer. It will bring down the world as we know it."

"So faith, whether in Christianity or other faiths is what truly creates a better world?" Sally was intrigued. Maria continued.

"Yes, genuine faith creates hope and love. Compassion for others. A world where all are valued and cared for. I don't mean religion like the Taliban or terrorist groups that claim to be religious, I mean genuine individuals that act in love because of their faith in a God."

A light began to dawn in Sam's mind. He spoke quietly and

nervously unsure of his thoughts.

"So an atheistic world would be a disaster for the poor, the disabled, and the vulnerable. It would be bad for the environment, for economics and global politics. It could lead to a global crisis and even a global war."

"Now you understand why it is so vital that we find John if he is real. Protect him from The Six and prevent a global meltdown. Christos sat back and sighed. "Can we do it?"

"I am going to try!" said Sam

"Me too," said Sally. "This is bigger than our safety. Lives depend on us!"

Sam went to call for the bill, but Maria stopped him.

"Sam, a guest in my home does not pay for their meal. You are family. Remember!" She smiled. The penny dropped.

"You're Maria! You own this taverna!"

"My friend Patrick, the English monk, is a regular here. We have spoken often of our interest in the Apostle. He is not so sure. But we are."

SEVENTEEN

The Chairman listened to his wife snoring as she lay beside him in their large detached house on an exclusive gated estate in North London. He sighed. She was gentle, kind and a good mother to their children. She was a necessity. A man in his position needed the stability of family life, the public demanded it. Her insistence that they attend the local parish church rankled with him. It stuck in his throat, but he played the part well. He thought of The Secretary and her lithe body straddling his. That was more like it. She was willing, she had no qualms, she was perfect. *Mind you,* he thought, *now that I've seen the HR member in person, I wouldn't mind a go with her too.* He made a mental note to hold a private meeting the next time The Six convened.

He got up, slipped on a dressing gown and wandered into his study. It was 4 am and the first reports from around the globe would be coming in. He was frustrated that the torture and execution of the priest had led to nothing. He was sure that damned priest knew something. His teams found no evidence in his apartment and his laptop was a dead end. *Why would that priest spend a lifetime researching, and hunting a man down if there were no truth to it? This John character had to be real. If he was, then I will be the one to destroy him and end the Christian faith once and for all!* The Chairman suddenly realised his heart rate was up and he was sweating.

Melanie Chambers stepped off the cut-price airline flight to Tel Aviv and boarded the bus to the terminal. It was hot and sticky and she needed a shower. The film crew were already here and had travelled ahead to Jerusalem to start filming background scenes. She would join them tomorrow.

"Look, it's Melanie Chambers!" A woman rushed over to

her beaming and scrambling for her mobile. "I love your programmes, Melanie. Can I call you Melanie? Please can we have a selfie? I'm a big fan." Another woman arrived dragging a cabin bag. Melanie forced a smile. *Remember, you're a celebrity, you're loved.* All she wanted was a shower and a cold glass of wine.

"Of course you can!" She stood between the two women and smiled as they both took selfies with her. The first woman continued to quiz her. "Are you here on holiday or are you filming? How exciting. Where is your crew?" Melanie responded politely and then excused herself and found a seat on the bus. She was already exhausted. She had been in Rome on assignment when her editor asked her to cover the murder of a Catholic Priest in the Vatican. It had made her trip complicated but she had managed her assignment and done a top quality news report from the Vatican. This was why Melanie Chambers was one of the UK's most loved reporters and journalists. She was a household name and her face was recognisable by most Brits. Melanie Chambers was riding the crest of her wave of success and she was not about to fall off. She was twenty-eight years old, highly intelligent, and fluent in three languages other than her native English. She was of average height, but that was all that was average about her. She was slim, beautiful with lightly tanned skin that contrasted against her shoulder-length straight blonde hair. Heads turned when she walked past. She had worked hard on her image, creating a persona of easy-going, yet insightful, fun-loving and compassionate. She was a top journalist, interviewer and television presenter. She was currently making a series of documentaries for a major terrestrial channel about the impact of tourism on the sacred sites of the world. She was on a whirlwind tour of all the major holy sites of the globe. It was bread-and-butter work and it gave her a chance to travel. Albeit on low-cost airlines. She deserved better, or so she thought.

Around the time Melanie was being accosted by selfie hunters,

Sam and Sally checked into the Waldorf Astoria in Jerusalem, a fourth-floor suite with a balcony. After showering and changing they sat in the terrace bar sipping champagne and scrolling through their iPads. Edna had recently found evidence of a cult of St John based in Jerusalem. Local newspapers were claiming that cult members were stating that St John the Apostle was alive and well. The journalists had dismissed their evidence as fanciful nonsense and reduced the stories to the 'weird and wonderful' section of the paper.

"This is worth investigating whilst we're here. I know you have book research to do, but it seems too much of a coincidence." Sally was fired up. The past few days on Patmos had changed her. Meeting Christos and Maria, hearing their story and seeing their passion had galvanised her.

"I agree," said Sam sipping on his champagne. "Let's spend a couple of days on my book, sightseeing and being tourists and then we can go hunting for John. If anyone is watching us, Christos will let us know." Christos had also travelled separately to Jerusalem and would shadow them. "Our guardian angel." Sally had quipped before they had sailed from Patmos.

EIGHTEEN

Five hooded figures appeared on screen; each in their own little box. The Secretary of the European region chaired the meeting. He was keen for the meeting to be brief. He was due at his other job in central London in just over two hours. He was agitated at the lack of action across all regions. There was still so much to do, so much chaos to bring, so much delusion to destroy. He was a man of action and slow considered actions frustrated him.

"Chairman for the Middle East, report on progress in destabilizing Gaza and Israel." His voice was clipped and revealed his frustration. The Middle East Chairman responded. Her voice was calming.

"Mister Chairman, we are making excellent progress. The recent explosions in Gaza blamed on Zionist settlers were in fact our doing. This has caused the Muslims in Gaza to respond. Missile attacks have become more frequent. We were also responsible for the settler shootings in Hebron. This has, of course, aroused more hatred between Jews and Arabs. Our agents in the Israeli political system have been successful in pushing forward an anti-Muslim agenda in the Knesset under the guise of Israeli citizenship. Some of the hard-line Zionist politicians are in fact Atomists and members of The Six whose aim is to bring about an atheist Israel and destroy both the Jewish faith and Muslims in Israel."

There were nods of approval from the other Chairmen.

"But what of this cult of St John? Israeli journalists report the growth of a new cult devoted to revealing the apostle John to be alive. How have you responded to this?" The Middle Eastern Chairman shuffled in her seat. It was clear she had not been expecting this.

"Mister Chairman," her voice now carried a force that was

missing previously. "There are more pressing events here in the region than a few old men believing a two-thousand-year-old man is alive." She almost sneered as she spoke. She was about to continue when the European Chairman almost shouted at his screen.

"I don't think you realise that if this two-thousand-year-old man IS alive then this is THE most significant event since the lies about the resurrection of Christ himself!" He paused to draw breath. "Proving this man to be real would destroy all other faiths and would cause civil unrest amongst the religious communities of the world. Islam would be dead; Hinduism would be dead... then if we kill him so would Christianity. Our mission would be complete." There was silence on the screen as the other Chairmen took in this information.

"Our priority must be to prove this man to be real and then kill him publicly. All regions are to devote maximum resources to this." The screens erupted with conversation and the chat box filled with comments.

"No more discussion!" He ended the meeting abruptly.

NINETEEN

Robert Frost worked in the Foreign Office. He had joined on leaving Cambridge with a first in International Relations. Now, twenty or so years later he was a senior civil servant and special advisor to several ministers in the Foreign Office. He had significant authority and was privy to a wealth of sensitive information relating to British affairs overseas. Frost took pride in his appearance. He kept himself fit and ensured he dressed in the best clothes. His blonde hair was just beginning to turn white but, in his eyes, it made him look distinguished and gave him an air of authority and wisdom. He stood in front of the long mirror in his office, lost in self-admiration. The phone rang and broke the spell. He stepped over to his desk, sat in the leather swivel chair and picked up the phone.

"Frost." His tone was professional. He listened to the voice on the end of the phone. "Yes Ma'am, at once. I will be with you as soon as the data is collated." He put the phone down and pressed a button to call his secretary who answered within one ring.

"Please could you collect and print all data on an organisation called The Six, mark it top secret for the Minister's eyes only and get it to me ASAP. Thank you." He replaced the receiver and sighed, wondering what the Secretary of State wanted with it. It puzzled him.

"But Minister, you can't seriously think that an organisation such as this suggests, actually exists?" Frost's voice clearly showed his contempt for the conclusions the security services had drawn. The Secretary of State for Foreign and Commonwealth Affairs clearly thought differently.

"Robert, I understand you think there are more urgent matters than this, but the intelligence is clear. It is suggesting that

The Six is a genuine threat to national security and to our relationships with our allies across the globe. I cannot afford to ignore it. If they were responsible for the spate of terror attacks and assassinations that we have seen recently, then we must act to seek them out and eradicate them. I will be instructing MI5 and 6. Although I expect they already have plans afoot. They may have to take matters into their own hands. That is if they can manage to work together." The minister sat back and flicked her hair from her eyes. She was in her mid-forties and still retained much of her youthful looks and charm. She smiled at Robert, knowing that Robert found her attractive, and she used it to her advantage. Robert did find her attractive but at the same time, he seethed inwardly, feeling emasculated by her authority over him.

"Yes, minister, I'll see to it that the relevant information is passed across to the Home Office. I take it you will be in touch with the security services." He worked hard to maintain a neutral tone. *Bitch! What does she know?*

TWENTY

The old city of Jerusalem was everything Sam and Sally had hoped it would be. For two days they explored it: the Via Dolorosa, The Western Wall, the Dome of the Rock, and the Church of the Holy Sepulchre. Sally took photos and Sam scribbled notes. They interviewed locals, priests, and worshippers, seeking to get a sense of the spirituality of the city and how locals understood its connection to Jesus. They regularly dropped in the name of John, just to see the reaction. On the second day, they got one. They were in the Bible Lands Museum on the west of the city interviewing one of the curators, an elderly woman in her mid-seventies. She had lived in the city all her life and worked at the Museum since it opened in the early nineties.

"John is an enigma," she said carefully in almost a whisper. They were sitting in the café of the museum; it was quiet as it was early in the day. "The legends and stories are strong and compelling." She sipped her coffee.

"But, you don't believe he is actually alive, that the legends are true, do you?" Sally leaned in across the table in a conspiratorial fashion. Sam watched the woman closely.

"You dear sweet thing. Do you still believe that what science tells you is always correct? Don't be so naïve. There is so much more to this world than that which science can explain. John is alive. He exists and my organisation have proof." She patted Sally's hand like a mother saying 'there, there' to her child. Sam became suddenly focused.

"Organisation?"

"Yes. My friends and I have spent years chasing John across the globe, trying to catch up with him, to make his presence known, to finally prove the reality of the Christian faith. If we could catch him, test his DNA and prove his identity then the world would have to acknowledge the existence of God and it would change the world." There was a sparkle in her eye. This was her passion, her life's work.

"So, where is he, then?" Sam tried to cover his excitement with an overly sarcastic tone. He didn't want the woman to realise they were that interested. She smiled and thought carefully before responding.

"Tonight, 8 pm at this address." She scribbled it on a napkin. "I will introduce you to the Cult of St John." She stood and held out her hand. "Thank you, Mr Tucker, Mrs Tucker. I hope you find everything you need for your book." She spoke loudly as if to emphasise the content of their conversation to anyone who might be eavesdropping, then turned and walked out leaving them to finish their coffee alone. A few tables away the hulky frame of Christos sat reading a newspaper.

The address was a large house in Kiryat Yearim just off the Jerusalem Tel Aviv highway. They arrived with five minutes to spare. It had a well-manicured garden with a fountain and a lawn on which you could putt. The house itself was quite modern and Sam noticed security cameras high up on the walls giving full coverage of the front. Before they even rang the bell the door opened and the familiar face of the curator let them in. As the door closed, a black four-wheeled drive truck pulled up on the road opposite and the shadowy figure of Christos sat and waited.

Sam and Sally entered a large sitting room, furnished in a modern style in keeping with the design of the house. A large Persian rug adorned the polished wooden floor and one piece of modern art hung on the wall. It was not to Sam's taste, it looked like someone had splashed paint pots randomly on a canvas. *Any idiot can do that.*

"Welcome, Mr and Mrs Tucker, we are so glad to have you here. My name is Jackson, Dennis Jackson and we are the Cult of St

John." He spread his hands out to include everyone else in the room. There were about eight mainly elderly, white Europeans. "I say, 'cult' we're not weird. Worshipping some goat or stuff like that. We're not into brainwashing or suicide pacts." He laughed at his own little joke. Sam and Sally just stood and stared. The people in the room introduced themselves. It was like meeting elderly relatives for the first time.

"Hello," Sam was a little bemused. He was expecting something sinister, more 'cultish.'

"Hi," said Sally smiling, trying to hide the fact she thought it was all highly amusing. This was like a nursing home convention.

"Sherry?" Dennis held up a bottle and glasses. "We always have a tipple before we get down to business. By the way, we have checked you out. We know you're not from the Israeli authorities. They see us as some kind of threat." He laughed as he spoke, as did several of the others. "We're just a bunch of good Christian folk who know St John is alive and want to find him to prove to the world that our religion is real and the others are false. We mean no harm. Please sit down." He handed them both a glass of sherry.

"May I ask a question?" Sally nervously raised her hand, as if she were in school.

"Of course my dear, go ahead." Dennis smiled politely.

"Surely, if you prove Christianity to be true, won't that cause massive unrest, leading to persecution of Christians as members of other faiths take…" she hesitated, trying to find the right word. "revenge?"

"In the short term, yes. But eventually, everyone would see the benefits and the world would come under the rule of Christ. Much better for the whole world!" Dennis spoke enthusiastically, seemingly unaware of the potential loss of life and chaos his ideas would bring. Sam nodded sagely as if agreeing, but inwardly his stomach churned. There was little difference between this group of enthusiastic Christians and 'The Six'. Both ideals would end in chaos.

"Doesn't the bible say in Revelation that Christ will reveal himself at the end times and reign over the world, why does he need you to help him?" Sally, like Sam had seen the inherent danger in their plan and wasn't about to keep quiet.

"We're not interfering. Who's to say that our actions aren't what God intends all along?" Dennis smiled again. Sam wanted to move the meeting along. He wanted to know if they knew where John was.

"I'm willing to search on your behalf and find John. I have the time and resources. If you share your evidence with me." The group of pensioners huddled and whispered as Sally and Sam sipped their sherry. Dennis eventually turned back to them and spoke.

"We agree, but when you find him, you bring him to us." Sam nodded non-committedly. It seemed to be enough for Dennis. He walked over to a desk in the corner of the room and took out a large ring binder. He handed it over to Sam. "This is a copy of all our research going back ten years. Our last sighting was in Berlin three months ago, but he slipped through our fingers."

An hour later, Sam and Sally walked down the path and onto the road. Christos was parked several yards up on the left-hand side. It was getting dark. As they climbed into the truck, three cars screeched around the corner. Two sealed off the road on either side of the house they had just been in the third drove up the drive. Masked men armed with machine guns got out. A burst of fire blew out the front door lock and they burst into the house. Sam, Sally and Christos looked on in horror. Moments later several more bursts of gunfire were heard and the gunmen returned dragging Dennis with them. He was bundled into the car which reversed off the drive at speed. All three cars drove off at pace.

"Shit! What the hell just happened?" Sam's face was pale. Sally's too. She just stared out of the window. Christos put the truck into gear and drove away, not too fast, as people we coming out of other houses to see what happened. He was careful not to draw attention to them. The wail of sirens could be heard approaching.

The three of them sat in the suite at the Waldorf Astoria, drinks in hand. Christos had driven them around the city to ensure they were not followed and to give them time to calm down. They were now trying to assess what had happened.

"This was not the Israelis, it's not their style. It could be Muslim extremists!" Christos was taking control. His experience keeping them calm. "However, I believe that this was The Six. It fits with what we already know."

Sally flipped open her laptop and opened her news app. There was a live feed covering it. "They're calling it a mass shooting of a religious nature." She said quietly. "The reporter is that woman off the TV… Melanie Chambers. How did she get here so quickly? She turned the screen to allow the other two to see. Melanie was speaking directly to the camera.

"It appears to be a massacre of a small cult called the 'Cult of St John.' They believe that the apostle John is still alive and are trying to find him. Witnesses say that several masked men drove up to the house broke in and shot them all. Taking one hostage. Three vehicles were seen driving off at speed." The three of them waited anxiously for any reference to a truck. There was none. They sighed.

Melanie continued. "It is believed that Muslim or Jewish extremists were responsible in order to prevent this group from locating the said apostle. This is an appalling act of violence on what appears to be a harmless group of pensioners with a few wild ideas."

"We have to get this data uploaded to Edna, see what she comes up with and get to Berlin as quickly as we can. If it is The Six behind this, then I expect they have the originals too." Sam had a new resolve. The events of the evening had not only shocked him but made him realise how serious The Six actually were. "We have to stop them."

"Oh my God! Dennis! I bet they have tortured him too like Luca." Sally put a hand up to her mouth. "If he talks, then they will know about us!"

"Let's pray that he doesn't." Christos swallowed the last of his whisky.

TWENTY-ONE

Berlin had been damp and dull and ultimately yielded limited fruit for Sam and Sally. Christos remained their shadow, constantly monitoring them from a safe distance, ensuring they were not being followed. As yet they were safe. The lead provided by Dennis in his folder of data pointed to a local Berliner named Johan Heiliger. He had become somewhat of a celebrity amongst the poor and homeless of Berlin. His tireless work every night providing food, clothing and company had soon come to the attention of the local churches and then the Television networks. A local Berlin News station had run a report on him and had remarked that his name really did reflect the idea of St John as Heiliger meant 'saint'. This had been picked up by the cult in Israel who had begun to research him, they were on the point of contact having made discreet enquiries with the local Berlin churches.

"I can't believe we missed him." They sat in Berlin's Brandenburg Airport in one of the many food outlets awaiting their flight to Gatwick. Sally was frustrated, she was keen to track this man down and hide him from the 'Six.' "He's been helping the poor in Berlin for a decade, why leave now? That's too much of a coincidence. Something must have spooked him."

"Perhaps he was warned in a dream by God to escape?" Sam was being facetious, recalling stories from his youth club days. He grinned at his wife. She smiled back.

"That's all very well, but if he is the apostle, then that is not all that far-fetched is it?" As soon as she said it, they both realised that it may well be true. If John was real, and it was Johan Heiliger, then perhaps God himself were protecting him.

"That does seem to be the pattern with all the possible sightings throughout history. Edna has collated a file of over one hundred 'Johns' who displayed Christian attributes, served the community for a while and then vanished. It seems there is evidence out there and it is pointing to the idea that Apostle John is real. Either that or all decent Christian men through history are called John!"

They had been to the local Berlin Lutheran Church aptly named Apostel-Johannes-Geimeindezentrum, or translated, John the Apostle Congregational Centre. It was a modern nineteen-seventies building of angular design. There they had spoken to the minister, Pastor David. He glowed with praise for Johan and his work, exclaiming how he was a loved and admired member of their congregation. But he had been out of town for a day or so, which was unusual as he never went anywhere, only to serve the poor in the city. Pastor David was keen to talk, assuming that he may get a mention in Sam's book. Sam had vaguely mentioned he was researching a book and the minister had assumed more than he should have. Sam chose not to correct him. No one seemed to know where Johan had gone. He had simply vanished.

As they sat discussing their missed opportunity and lack of progress, the TV on the back wall that usually displayed a silent rolling news programme burst into life. The waitress had turned it up. There on the screen was a picture of the outside of the Apostel-Johannes-Geimeindezentrum church with a reporter outside. There were gasps from some of the German-speaking travellers as they tuned into the report. Sam and Sally both looked up and tried to fathom out what was going on. Neither of them spoke German.

"Look," said Sally and pointed to the screen. "There in the background, isn't that Melanie Chambers? What's she doing there? I thought she was in Israel?"

"Good grief, she gets around. I wonder what's going on. That's where we were the other day." Sam motioned to one of the waitresses and asked what was happening on the TV.

The young woman spoke haltingly. "Someone has tried to

assassinate the congregation of the church as they came out from worship." She was clearly upset. "I cannot believe it, that this would happen here in Berlin. The reporter says it was a rival Christian group that opposed some of their beliefs. To me that is crazy. That's not Christian that is madness." There was a tear in her eye. Sally was moved and stood up and hugged the waitress.

"I am so sorry this has happened."

"Danke!" The waitress moved off, wiping a tear away.

Sam and Sally looked at each other knowingly.

"Why would The Six do this? It makes no sense. I thought they wanted John alive. Why kill those around him?" Sally was genuinely bemused and upset.

"I guess it fits with their bigger plan, to undermine religion and portray it as violent, hateful and bigoted. Maybe they want to send a warning to John. To let him know they are after him."

"Won't that just make him go into hiding? Move on somewhere else? It looks as if he's already jumped ship!" She slumped back in her chair.

"The trail will go cold. We have no idea where John went. We will have to start all over again." Sam was equally frustrated. "Let's just get home, I can get on with my book and we can let Edna sift through all the extra data. Maybe something will turn up."

TWENTY-TWO

The September evening sun was still warm; it had been a hot day in Sussex. Sam and Sally sat with their friends and estate managers Ian and Kelly, around an outdoor dining table laden with food and drink. They were on a porticoed patio at the rear of the main farmhouse. As they ate and drank together as friends, they also discussed business.

"The Farm shop is up and running and the work on the glamping site has begun. But Kelly will fill you in on that." He smiled at his wife. Ian was tall and muscular, an outdoor person whose skin was tanned from years working the land in various capacities. "I've employed a couple of students part-time and a local woman to manage the shop. They're doing well. We've been very busy since opening and other local producers are keen to use our shop, so we're buying in more stock. We've even got a licence to sell alcohol. The local microbreweries are keen to use us."

"That's great Ian; you have done us proud while we've been abroad. Thank you." Sam was impressed by his friend and grateful to him. He was good to have around.

"Kelly, what are all those diggers in the west field?" Sally knew but wanted Kelly to explain her work as Ian had done.

"Well, permission came through from the council for the camping site, including four permanent huts or pods, a shower and toilet block, and electric hook-ups and water for 20 pitches. The builders began two weeks ago and have laid out the main paths and dug out trenches for sewage and the like already. Work on the construction of the shower block begins next week and the time scale is we should be ready to open for the spring next year."

Sally raised a glass. "To camping and farming!" They all clinked glasses and laughed together.

"To friends, to trust and to the truth." Sam raised a glass again. There was some hesitation and then they all joined in.

"That was an odd toast, Sam, what do you mean, trust and the truth?" Ian was intrigued.

"Well, Sal and I haven't just been on holiday…" With that, Sam and Sally recounted everything that had happened while they had been away.

"Bloody hell," said Kelly, "it sounds like an Agatha Christie!"

"That's what I said to Sam!" Sally laughed.

"But it is genuine and it is dangerous. These people, whoever they are, The Six, are crazy and will stop at nothing to achieve their goals." Sam had become a little more sombre. "We wanted you to know in case people come asking about it. Or something bad happens. You will know. If you want to leave and move on in order to keep safe. We will understand."

Ian and Kelly looked at each other. Kelly stood up, her shoulder-length black hair tied in a ponytail, bobbing a little. She was shorter than Ian but equally tanned and toned due to her outdoor life. She moved around the table and stood behind Sam and Sally. She leaned over them, placed her arms around them, and whispered in their ears.

"We're not going anywhere. We are your friends. No, we are family. More than friends. We are here for you."

"You trusted us enough to let us loose with your business and you trusted us to let us in on this mystery. We won't let you down." Ian raised a glass. "To John, wherever he is! If he is!"

TWENTY-THREE

The chairman looked across at the woman lying next to him. His personal meeting with the HR representative of The Six had gone better than he had hoped. Not only had she been willing to sleep with him but her enthusiasm and athletic body were a dream. *Hedonism is the way, do what you want with whom you want. Enjoy life, there are no limits.* His thoughts wandered back to the bigger picture and mission of the 'Six.' There had been several more attacks on religious venues, and more 'accidents' involving religious leaders. Fighting between religious denominations was on the increase and public opinion was slowly turning. He now needed a route into the institutions of government and social institutions like the media. To infiltrate them and promote his anti-religious agenda would bring about a shift in society that would eventually change public opinion, create new laws and ultimately remove religion from society altogether. He had seen this working well with other pressure groups such as vegans and environmentalists. *Surely the same would work with our vision?*

The athletic woman stirred and the Chairman turned to look at her. He thought briefly about his wife with a small pang of guilt, but it passed quickly as she wrapped her arms around him again and began to explore him.

Since their return to the UK Sam and Sally had identified numerous religious-inspired hate crimes across the globe. Churches in India were set on fire and blamed on Hindus. Aggression was rising against Rohingya Muslims inspired by the Buddhist government in Burma. Sectarian violence in Northern Ireland was again rearing its ugly head. All over the world instances of violence involving religion seemed unconnected, but Sam and Sally knew better. They sat and watched the news as another report of an explosion at a London mosque was reported.

"Why don't we ask her to help us?" Sally pointed to the screen. "She must have more contacts and be able to ask more questions than us." There on the screen outside a west London Mosque stood Melanie Chambers, reporting for a major news channel.

" …it seems the attack was intended to harm the local congregation at Friday prayers, and it seems they have succeeded. Several have been killed including some women and children. An anonymous call to the BBC apparently from the bomber said this and I quote. 'The scourge of Islam in the UK is becoming too great to bear any longer. It is time for all true Christians to rise up and slaughter the infidel just as we did in the time of the Crusades. A new crusade is beginning. We must restore Britain to its Christian heritage.' The message is apparently from an extreme right-wing Christian group called 'Messengers of the Last Days.' Police are currently investigating this group and are expected to make arrests shortly. I am joined here by Yousef…" Melanie's voice was calming and concerned at the same time, her screen presence was captivating. Sam watched closely.

"What do you think?" Sally waited for Sam to respond. "Well?"

"Eh? Sorry I wasn't listening." He was still staring at the TV following Melanie's report. Sally leaned across him in front of the TV.

"Hello! I'm here, your wife. Stop ogling that reporter." She waved and Sam snapped out of his spell.

"I was just…"

"I know what you were just doing… Yes, she is pretty and charming. But she doesn't love you like I do! Now get your brain out of your trousers and concentrate. Should we get her to help us? Mind you, you'd be no good, you'd just dribble in front of her." Sally was beginning to enjoy ribbing her husband.

"Okay, okay I get it. Sorry. Do I make a fuss when you ogle Brad Pitt?" Sam winked at his wife. "I don't know. How would we contact her? Why would she be interested? How do we know we can trust her?" Sam was reluctant to open it out to others but saw the value in having a proper reporter with access to other sources.

"Sam, she is an investigative journalist, she's doing a series on religion. It's being advertised on the TV. She must have some insight that could help us. I don't mean tell her about John and The Six directly but give her some hints, and get her on our side. Why don't we ask Christos, what he thinks?" She leaned in and kissed her husband.

"Okay, but if he disagrees we knock it on the head and go it alone."

"You can use your research and book as a way to meet her. Invite her down here."

TWENTY-FOUR

Sam's publisher and Melanie Chamber's agent had struck a deal for one interview with the prospect of Sam appearing in one of Melanie's series of religious documentaries. Now they sat in one of Claridge's restaurants, the Foyer and Reading Room. Sam and Sally had booked in for a short city break to include the interview with Melanie Chambers. In the centre of the room, a Chihuly sculpture hung like a chandelier and the walls were covered with art deco mirrors giving the room a larger feel. A pianist played smooth, classic tunes on a grand piano.

All three sat around in luxurious green velvet chairs enjoying a Claridge's afternoon tea. They chatted politely for a while about Melanie's work and Sam's book, Sam speaking enthusiastically about his love of archaeology and his interest in biblical history. Melanie Chambers listened attentively as any good journalist would. After about thirty minutes the conversation changed.

"So, Sam, let's be honest, why did you both want to meet me? A deal about your book and appearance in a documentary could have been done via our agents. There is something more you are not telling me. Or are you just a crazed fan who wants a selfie and an autograph?" She laughed at her own joke.

For the first time, Sally made a meaningful contribution to the conversation. "You're very perceptive Melanie. There is another issue that is on our minds. Something that we think you may be able to help with." Melanie Chambers looked at Sally and for the first time really noticed her beauty and her strength of character. The tone of her voice carried authority, not desperation. She was impressed.

"Go on, I'm listening." Melanie leaned forward slightly to emphasise that she was interested.

"As you know, Sam has been researching his book and as part of it, we have travelled to destinations in Eastern Europe and the Middle East. Religious convictions are strong in this region and we have also noticed a spike in religious hate crimes across the globe and in particular in that region. We wondered if they were all random and disconnected or if there was some coordination as if a darker force were in play." Melanie's interest was piqued. She leaned closer, and her eyes widened.

"Really, what makes you say so? Can you give me specifics? What is it you would like me to do?" Her usual calm voice displayed a sense of excitement. Her heart rate was slightly raised.

Sam continued. "Well, that massacre in Jerusalem of all those pensioners. They belonged to a cult linked to the apostle John. Then there was the one in Berlin, all worshippers at the Apostel-Johannes-Gemeindezentrum church. It's just they are both connected with John." Sam paused to let Melanie take it on. When she spoke she was less enthusiastic.

"What's your point? I covered those stories, but there was no connection. Different groups have claimed responsibility."

"We know," said Sam looking at Sally for support, "but what if that is a lie and something bigger is going on?"

"Such as?" She held out her hands in an open, questioning gesture.

"What if someone or a group of people want to destabilise countries or economies, what better way to do so than to stir up religious hatred between peoples? Religion is the one thing that people get fired up about." Sam then reeled off a string of other examples of recent religious hate crimes. "Look at how all these disrupted local economies and caused unrest. Even for a short while."

Melanie sat back in her chair and took a sip of her champagne. "Maybe there's something in it, maybe not. It all sounds like a James Bond plot."

"Please Melanie, all we're asking is that you ask around. Use your contacts, dig about a little. It is what you do for a living." Melanie liked Sam, he was handsome and fit for his age. He had a kind nature. *I wouldn't mind him in my bed.* She was not surprised by the thought. She often had them about people she met. Sometimes she acted on it. *You'd be a challenge, that wife of yours is feisty and you clearly love her.* She leaned over and took Sam's hand. She smiled seductively at him.

"I'll do it for you, I will check it out." She squeezed his hand and winked.

"Thank… Thank…" Sam stumbled over his words, suddenly unsure of himself. The fact that Melanie Chambers was coming on to him.

Sally quickly intervened. She stood, "I think what my husband is trying to say is thank you very much. It is much appreciated." Her tone was firm and indicated that Sam was not on the market for a new woman. She stuck out her hand to shake Melanie's who took it. The shake was firm, maybe a touch too firm. Sam stood and held out his hand too, having recovered from his momentary confusion. Melanie leaned in and kissed him on the cheek.

"Bye Sam, darling. I'll be in touch." Melanie turned and strode off, and the interview was terminated.

"Bitch." Sally whispered.

"What, that's a bit harsh, she was only flirting…" Sam was still a little flushed by his experience of meeting the beautiful and enchanting celebrity that was Melanie Chambers, and the fact she appeared to fancy him.

"Get up Sam, follow me." There was a serious tone in her voice. She held out her hand for Sam to take.

"Where are we going? What's wrong?"

"I'm taking you up to our room to show you why you don't need to be interested in celebrities."

From the corner of the room, a woman appeared to be taking pictures of the art deco mirrors and other features of the room. To all intents and purposes, Sam and Sally accidentally photobombed her shots.

An hour later, they lay naked under the duvet of the super king-size bed in their suite. Their clothes were strewn over the floor.

"Thank you," said Sam with a big smile on his face.

"You're welcome." Sally leaned in and kissed her husband on the cheek.

"But, just to make sure…" Sam rolled over and straddled his wife pinning her arms against the bed.

"Oh, okay, if you insist," she giggled.

TWENTY-FIVE

Johan Heiliger sat on the train in London's Victoria Station. It had several minutes to go before departure. Passengers were arriving and finding seats and the train was quickly filling up as commuters began to head home. Johnan looked out of the window at the platform and allowed his mind to drift. It had been an arduous journey from Berlin. His passport and German identification card were with him but he wanted to travel discreetly. There were always means of travelling if you knew how to avoid the borders. He didn't like deceiving others, it went against his beliefs, but there were always times when it was necessary. This was one of them. He wasn't sure what had led him to leave Berlin, it was just a sense of unease. He had mourned and wept after he had seen the news of the attack on his former church, so many friends killed or injured. The attack had validated his sense of unease and made him wary. It had been many years since he had felt the need to flee and hide away until danger passed, and even more since he had been in England. He knew it was time for a change. Johan sat back closed his eyes and felt the train pull out from the station and make its way towards the south coast of England.

"Sir, sir. You can't stay on the train, it terminates here." The guard was gently shaking Johan.

He opened his eyes abruptly and sat up. "It's okay sir, you've been asleep. You need to get off the train. It terminates here. Is this your bag?" The guard pointed to a rucksack on the seat next to him. Johan nodded.

"Sorry, I hadn't realised how tired I was." He sat up and caught his reflection in the train window. For a moment, it startled him and then he realised and smiled. He stood up, stretched and picked up his rucksack.

"Thank you. Sorry for being a nuisance." Johan noticed his voice was a little croaky and not its usual strong accent. Perhaps he was coming down with something.

"No worries mate. I just didn't want you to wake up halfway back to London." Johan walked down the carriage toward the door, pressed the button and stepped off the train. Moving past the ticket barrier he entered the main concourse of Eastbourne station. It was a large Victorian building, a remnant of the expansion of the town way back when the Industrial Revolution allowed people to travel to the seaside for holidays. He stepped out into the street and blinked in the strong autumn sunshine. A sign read "Welcome to Eastbourne, Suntrap of the South." *Well, that's certainly true.* He walked across the road and headed for the main shopping centre where he could see a coffee shop. He needed to get his bearings and think. The journey had changed him and he had woken up feeling different. He needed time to assimilate it and decide on a new course of action. He ordered a flat white and sat in a window seat looking out at the traffic. He sat for an hour nursing his drink before deciding he needed to sleep on it. He headed up towards the seafront, passing numerous restaurants and bars on the way. He hadn't realised how hungry he was. He stopped at a small Greek restaurant and enjoyed a mezze platter and a glass of red wine. By the time he found a small hotel just off the seafront that was quiet and low-cost, it was getting late. A plan was formulated, a new start, a new name a new identity.

At the same time as Johan stepped off the train in Eastbourne, Robert Frost received an offer he could not turn down.

"Yes, sir, it would be an honour. I can move across to Downing Street within twenty-four hours, sir." Frost's voice was full of pride. His dream was coming true. More influence more power, more status. The Prime Minister's personal aide in Downing Street. Access all areas.

"The Secretary of State highly recommends you, Robert. She trusts you implicitly. It will mean more hours, unsocial hours and time away from your family. I know you are a family man. Will this be acceptable?" The Prime Minister's voice showed compassion and concern.

"My wife will understand. There will be no problem, I assure you. Let me make a call and I will confirm within the hour." The call ended and Robert Frost sat back in his leather chair and smiled the smile of a man who has just won the jackpot. He slipped his mobile out of his pocket and flicked through his contacts. After a short call, he once again sat back and smiled. *All sorted.* He pressed a button on his phone and spoke to his secretary.

"Pack up the office, we're moving to Downing Street."

Frost sat back in his chair and reflected on his rise to success. Having left his private school with excellent grades and spent three years at Cambridge studying international relations, he decided to join the Civil Service. His rise to the top had been meteoric compared to the usual slow, plodding progress that some take. A few lies and half-truths had not hindered him so far. The sale of his father's home had brought him significant wealth, which he had invested wisely. He was now a multi-millionaire which of course his wife knew nothing about. He sighed a contented sigh. Life was good and only going to get better.

The Chairman was in a good mood. He had slept with two of the females on the board of the European 'Six', the third was too old and did not interest him. However, he was still intrigued by the Chairman of the Middle East 'Six.' He would like to get her into bed and satisfy himself with her. The Zoom meeting was progressing well when an image popped up on his screen. Two faces. Clandestine photographs taken from a discreet distance. The Secretary spoke, her voice silky smooth and suggestive. The Chairman was momentarily distracted by the memory of her naked body on his.

"It has come to our attention that these two, Sam and Sally Tucker have been asking questions about some of our recent exploits and are making connections. They have even enlisted the help of an investigative journalist named Melanie Chambers."

The Chairman interrupted his Secretary. "Melanie Chambers, the TV presenter?"

"Yes, her indeed!"

"Sam Tucker, you say. What does he do for a living? Why is he snooping?" The Chairman looked closely at the photographs, inspecting them.

"He's an Estate Agent and owns a small chain of shops in Sussex. She's an accountant. They are doing well and have a farm in a village called Alfriston. He also writes history books, Biblical history. He's just finishing one about St John." The Secretary concluded her summary.

"Interesting, but nothing for us to worry about. Make sure they don't get any closer but don't harm them. We don't need unnecessary blood spilt. I don't want my mood being spoilt by news of the death of two nosey busybodies."

"Understood. Let me deal with it, Chairman. I know how to handle it discreetly." There was a hint of menace in the Secretary's voice.

TWENTY-SIX

Robert Frost sat in his new office in Downing Street and enjoyed a moment of calm before he began his new role as a personal aide to the Prime Minister. He had brought his secretary with him, an efficient young man whose ambition was as great as his. Perhaps he would be useful in the future if he wanted to progress even further. Robert was good at using people in such a way that they never quite realized when they had been taken for a ride. He had learned at an early age not to trust anyone but to use them for his own advantage. His thoughts drifted back to the dark times as a child when he had suffered abuse at the hands of a priest, someone he should have been able to trust, someone whom everyone believed to be genuine, but he knew was evil. It had taken all his strength to entice the priest back to abuse him one more time. But this time he was ready. He had hidden a tape recorder in his room at the boarding school and recorded the abuse. In triumph, he handed it over to his father to give to the police. Instead, his weak father had taken it to the school and tried to reason with them. The priest had subsequently moved on and Robert was moved to a different boarding school. No charges were ever brought against the priest or the school. As a result, three things changed in Robert's life. The first was that his love for his father died. Hate grew quickly and thoughts of vengeance filled his young mind. They were finally fulfilled when he was twenty and an 'unknown assailant' broke into his house in an attempted burglary and stabbed his father to death. The second was that he chose to live in a way that gave him pleasure and never allowed anyone to use him again. Finally, he vowed that he would do all in his power to reveal the hypocrisy in religious belief. He became an ardent atheist.

The phone startled him and brought him back to the present.

"Sir," said Tim his secretary, "the police are here. Two officers are downstairs. They need to speak to you. They have clearance from security. Shall I get them brought up?"

"Of course, send them straight up."

Ten minutes later, Robert sat on the Chesterfield sofa in his office holding a mug of tea. The two CID officers sat opposite in leather Sherlock-style chairs.

"I can't believe it," he kept repeating the phrase. "Are you sure it is her?"

"Yes, sir we are. She was carrying her driving licence in her purse. We will need you to identify her formally of course." Robert appeared to be in shock. He sat there repeating the same phrase over again. "Are you sure?"

Robert's wife had been attacked in the street by a man of Middle Eastern origin wearing traditional Arab dress with his face covered by a Keffieh. He had wielded a machete and slashed at Suzanne Frost several times calling out "Allah hu Akbar, God is great, death to Christians!" Suzanne Frost had bled to death on the pavement whilst the assailant fled.

By the time the evening news came on, Suzanne and Robert's faces were known nationally.

"My God, that's Bobby Frost, I'm sure of it. I know him. We used to hang about together when we were teenagers. He lived in a big house down the road from me." Sam sat up in his armchair and took a longer look at the news.

"What, you mean you and him were mates? He's a top guy in the civil service. Blimey!" Sally seemed impressed.

"Well, he wasn't then, was he? Poor bloke that must be awful. That's the second tragedy to hit him. His dad was murdered in his own home when Bobby was twenty. That's the last time I saw him at his dad's funeral." They sat and watched the news story being told and as they did, a gradual realisation came over them. Was this the work of The Six?

"I have to contact him, let him know. Maybe he could help?"

"Sam, his wife's just been hacked to death! He's in no state to give anyone help."

Over the next few days, Robert Frost made several TV appearances on the news, appealing for calm in the public, not to seek revenge on the Muslim community but to seek forgiveness. But the murder seemed to have stirred up the right-wing nationalists who were using it as an excuse to attack Muslims and mosques. There was a significant amount of civil unrest.

The Chairman sat in his favourite chair late at night, sipping whisky. He watched Robert Frost, the new Prime Minister's aide on the news appealing for calm and thought to himself *the more he tries to stop it the more it will stir up hatred*. He smiled, the death of Suzanne Frost was worth it. His phone buzzed. The Secretary was on her way to see him. He smiled lasciviously at the thought of a few hours of pleasure with her.

TWENTY-SEVEN

Sam watched Sally and Kelly jog back across the yard. He knew he needed to get back to a regime of fitness, but he felt consumed by The Six and how to defeat them or at least expose them. He rifled through the post and saw a letter with the Downing Street crest on the envelope. Intrigued he opened it and read the letter. He shook his head in disbelief, sat down, sipped his coffee and waited for Sal to come in. He could see her chatting with Kelly and grew slightly impatient. He was keen to share the content of the letter with Sal.

"Shit!" said Sally, more than surprised by the letter she held in her hand. Sam had thrust the letter into her hand as soon as she had come through the back door into the boot room. Ronnie the sheepdog fussed around her wanting to know what the excitement was about.

"I can't believe it; why would he invite you? You don't even know him anymore." Sally was as perplexed as Sam by the formal invitation to Suzanne Frost's funeral at St Mary's Church Hamsted. "How does he even know where we live? This is a bit strange don't you think? You wanted to go to the funeral and all of a sudden you get a formal invite! It's a bit like how we all think our smart speakers are listening to us!" Sam laughed but inside there was uncertainty. Sally was right.

"I wonder if my mum gave him the address. Remember, she still lives in the house where I grew up. As far as I know, Robert's mum and my mum are still friends."

"What, she still lives in the house where her husband was murdered? That's a bit creepy. I'd want to move." Sally pulled a distasteful face.

"Mum said she didn't want to be beaten by the murderer. She wouldn't give in. But Bobby insisted she move. He bought her a bungalow and then sold his Dad's house that had been left to him, rather than his mum."

"Harsh," said Sally. "He sounds like a selfish bastard!" Sally refocused and returned to the letter.

"We still haven't resolved the issue of why Bobby wants you at the funeral. Like you said, you haven't seen him for twenty years." Sally couldn't let it drop. "It just seems odd."

"Agreed, it is weird, but the upside is, we wanted to go and I might be able to arrange a meeting with Bobby and talk about The Six. He must have heard of them being the PM's aide." Sam was feeling upbeat. "I'll make your breakfast whilst you shower. Ten minutes?" Sally smiled; "Fifteen." She turned and left the room. Sam followed her with his eyes and smiled at his wife. He always did.

Johnny Saint sat in a small independent coffee shop off the main shopping street in Eastbourne. He was finding it increasingly difficult to start over, create a new identity for himself. Fortunately, he had an existing bank account and NI number from a previous time he had lived in the UK. He had wisely kept it going and occasionally used the account to prevent it from being closed by the bank. He had renewed his British Passport at the Embassy in Berlin the previous year, however, he was beginning to be concerned by the date of birth it revealed. He hoped no one looked too closely. Johnny Saint was alive and kicking, for how long he did not know. He was still surprised that no one he had met in the UK had realised that if you switched his names around it made Saint John. He silently prayed. *How much longer Lord? The world is a mess. Come, Lord Jesus, come!"*

He sipped his coffee and began searching for affordable accommodation in the area as well as a job to give him credibility if he were to continue the mission his Lord had given him. Johnny Saint loved the Lord Jesus with all his heart. Jesus was his friend and had been ever since he had become a believer all those years ago down by the lake where he used to fish. His phone pinged and a news flash appeared. The funeral of Suzanne Frost, murdered by Muslim extremists was being held tomorrow. He read the story with interest and wondered if this was just another example of persecution of God's children, as foretold by Jesus himself. He was saddened by the story and decided he would go and pay his respects along with the thousands of others expected to line the roads outside the Hamstead church.

TWENTY-EIGHT

There was a heavy police presence at the church. The roads surrounding St Mary's were cordoned off and crowds stood behind barriers. Flowers of remembrance, given by the public, were laid out at the entrance to the church. Sam and Sally were shown to seats near the back and they sat and watched as the Prime Minister and several cabinet members arrived. Security was tight and Sam noticed armed police as well as members of the security services hovering discreetly around the 18th century church. The church itself was designed in a classical style with vaulted ceilings and white stone pillars inlaid with gold filigree. A balcony surrounded the nave on three sides and on the left as you looked toward the altar was a huge pipe organ surrounded by dark-panelled wood; it reminded Sam of the church that was used in the film *Four Weddings and a Funeral*.

When the organ began to play Chopin's funeral march, the congregation quickly settled and the coffin was carried slowly up the central aisle. Robert Frost and his son and daughter walked slowly behind. The teenage children hand in hand. Sam noticed the stoic look on Robert Frost's face and recalled him as a teenager, renouncing religion as evil. What had brought him back to the faith? The service progressed as only funerals could. Robert Frost's two children both gave moving tributes to their mother. Tears were shed. Then Frost himself gave a eulogy to his wife. As Sam listened to his old friend remembering his wife, it seemed to him soulless and lacking in emotion. He whispered to Sally.

"It's as if he didn't love her, she was just there."

"He's just trying to be brave and hold it together. I couldn't do what he's doing." Sally responded. She squeezed her husband's hand to remind him of their love, in case he had forgotten.

There was a short private committal in the graveyard whilst the remaining mourners made their way to Westminster Hall in the Palace of Westminster where a reception was to take place. As Sam and Sally stepped out into the autumn sunshine and down the steps of the church Sam scanned the crowd. There were hundreds of well-wishers and mourners sharing in the grief of a family who had so brutally lost a wife and mother. There were also some opportunist protesters from the far right with banners that suggested that all other faiths were wrong and that Jesus would smite the infidels. Sam's focus was drawn to a man who appeared to be in his late sixties, strong and fit, with a face that had experienced a wide variety of life experiences. For a second, the two men locked their gaze and Sam was transfixed. There was something about him. He couldn't place it. Something vaguely familiar.

"Sam, come on, what are you staring at?" Sally was two steps below him her hand still in his. They were stretched apart. "Why have you stopped?" Sam looked at his wife and smiled apologetically.

"Sorry, I thought I saw someone I knew." He turned back towards where the man had been standing. He was no longer there. He shook his head. He caught up with his wife and they made their way to Hamstead tube station.

"Who did you see?" Sally asked, "Anyone I know?"

"I'm not sure, it was an older man, he looked vaguely familiar, but I can't place him."

"That happened to my dad once," said Sally. "He was in a pub listening to a band when he thought a celebrity walked in and stood by the bar. He was convinced he was famous."

"Was he?" replied Sam interested in the story.

"No! He went and asked him. It turned out he was my Dad's optician. He just didn't recognise him out of context! He knew he was familiar but couldn't work out why." Sally laughed as she recounted the family tale. Sam chuckled too, but he was certain he knew that man from somewhere. *It will come to me when I least expect it.* He thought.

"Sam Tucker, I didn't know whether you would get my invitation. I wasn't sure where you were. But my secretary came up trumps." Robert Frost bypassed the extended hand that Sam held out and went in for a hug. He held his old friend tight. "Thank you for coming. I didn't know if you would remember me. I just recall how good you were to support me after my father was killed. I felt I needed an old friend around." Robert Frost turned to Sally.

"This must be your lovely wife. She's gorgeous, how did you manage to trap her?" He moved swiftly in and kissed Sally on the cheek and held her close and slightly too tight for just a second too long. A chill went down Sally's spine the moment she was released.

"A pleasure to meet you, Robert. I am so sorry for your loss." She motioned to the two teenagers who were engaged in polite conversation with the Prime Minister. "How are they holding up, it must be dreadful?"

"They're strong," he smiled. "They have all the support they need back at their schools." The comment puzzled Sally. She was about to question it when Sam took over.

"And how are you bearing up? Do you need any help? Is there anything I can do?" Sam didn't really know what to say, but it seemed the right thing.

"I'm fine, bearing up." Robert smiled a forced smile. One that all grieving people do at funerals.

"It seems you found your faith. That must be a help?" Sam was trying to look for some positives.

"What, that? No. That was my wife; she was into all that stuff.

Not for me. You remember what happened to me. I'd never trust a religious person again." Sam nodded sagely, remembering the abuse he had been told about when Robert was a kid.

Frost ended the conversation quickly. "Let's meet up, and reconnect We have a lot to discuss." He handed Sam a business card. "I must circulate, do the rounds." He smiled as if this were a business conference and he had arranged a meeting with a client.

"Well, that was all a bit odd!" Sam followed Robert Frost with his eyes as he made his way to his children ushered them out of the Prime Minister's presence and took their place.

"He gives me the creeps," said Sally, giving a mock shiver.

"What do you mean?"

"That hug he gave me was too keen, too close and too long. And what was all that about his kids? Sounds like he's shipping them back to school tomorrow! What does he mean by 'never trusting a religious person again'?" They sat down at a table with plates of food and two large glasses of wine and Sam retold Bobby Frost's story, the public school, the abuse by the priest and the school's failure to do anything about it.

By the time they left Westminster Hall, the sun was fading and rush hour had begun in earnest. Sam and Sally decided to walk back to their hotel. Sam had chosen the Great Scotland Yard hotel, as a fun place to stay. Converted from the old Scotland Yard building it had a grandiose style that reflected the historic nature of the building. It was only half a mile or so from Westminster. They walked hand in hand along the Victoria Embankment towards Charing Cross Station. As they turned up Northumberland Avenue they saw a woman walking towards them. Her left arm in a sling. She looked a little unsettled and nervous, looking around as if being followed.

"That's Mel!" Said Sally. She ran forward toward her, forgetting the earlier mistrust and the flirtatious nature she had tried to impose on her husband.

"Mel, are you okay? What's happened?" Sally stood in front of her and placed her hands on her shoulders. Mel was crying, her shoulders shaking. Sam arrived and repeated the questions. Mel began to explain but Sam stopped her.

"Wait, let's get you back to our hotel. We can have a drink and you can tell us what's happened." They shepherded Mel around the corner to the hotel and headed straight for the bar. Once settled in comfy leather armchairs with drinks in hand, Mel began to tell her story. She spoke hesitantly and tearfully.

"I'd just got back from work. I'd dumped my bag and slipped my shoes off and went straight into the kitchen of my flat to put the kettle on. When I came out into the lounge, it was there on the wall daubed in red paint. *Back off! 6.* It was then I realised the place was a mess. My desk and files were strewn everywhere. I screamed and dropped my tea on the floor. Just then I was grabbed from behind and a knife held at my throat…" She began to sob again as she recounted the trauma.

"Oh, my God!" Sally held her hand to her mouth.

"Take your time, Mel. It's okay. Have you told the police?" She nodded.

"Yes, I reported it, but that's not the end. The man threatened to kill me and anyone else who tried to find out about The Six. He made it perfectly clear he meant business." She slipped her arm out of the sling and gingerly pulled up her sleeve to reveal a large plaster and bandage. "He carved a six in my arm." She burst out crying again. Sam looked up at Sally and noticed the colour had drained from her cheeks. Sam too felt a little nauseous.

"Bloody hell, that's insane." Sam could feel the adrenaline beginning to flow and his heart rate increase, a mixture of anger and fear. Mel continued to tell of her encounter with the police and her desire to warn them. "I tried texting but you didn't respond. So I tracked you down." Sam fished his phone from his pocket and saw a series of unanswered texts from Melanie Chambers.

"We're so sorry," said Sally, almost crying herself. "We were at the big funeral, at Westminster, Robert Frost's wife."

Mel looked up, her make-up streaked with tears. "I know, that's how I found you."

"Look, Mel, stay here tonight, I'm sure they have a room, I'll pay. Then tomorrow we can go back and sort your flat out, okay." Sam looked at his wife just to make sure she was happy with the suggestion he had made. Sally nodded and recognised true compassion in her husband.

"Poor Mel, that must have been awful." They sat in bed in their deluxe room. "It just shows how dangerous The Six really are. Perhaps we're in too deep. Mel only found out a bit about them and she was nearly killed." Sally's tone was anxious.

"True, but we now know something about who the members of The Six are." Sam was excited by the news of Mel's discovery. Mel had shared some snippets of information she had discovered. "Look, we now know a young, budding actress is one of them."

"Actor," Sally corrected. "They're all called actors now, regardless of their gender."

"Whatever!" Sam shrugged, it wasn't that important. "Potato, tomato…"

Sally looked at him and guffawed. "Potato, potato" changing the emphasis as she spoke. "Not Potato tomato. Idiot!" They both laughed but then Sam continued.

"Seriously, an actor, a high-ranking army officer, two CEOs of international industry, an MP and a Head Teacher from a public school. This is huge. Look at the power they have to influence, cover things up, misdirect and hide the truth."

"Where did she get this from? Luca seemed to think the security services knew nothing, how come she finds this out in a few days?"

"I dunno, it's her job, she investigates stuff. If it's true, then we have something to go on. To take it further."

"I suppose so, but it seems too easy."

"Maybe she's just good at her job. What about those two guys who broke the Watergate scandal back in the Seventies? Good journalism. It goes on all the time. You can't not trust her 'cause she flirted with me."

"I do trust her; she nearly got killed for it. I do like her, but it just seems odd, that's all. What if she gets attacked again?"

"Look I'll ask Edna to do a search and see what she comes up with. Can she corroborate anything Mel has told us? I'll ask Christos and Maria to come over. They can shadow her for a week or two, to make sure she is okay. They can stay with us too. It will be like a holiday reunion. Now let's not waste this lovely hotel bed." With that, he flicked off the light and snuggled down next to his wife.

TWENTY-NINE

The Chairman was exhausted; his day had been busy but he had one more job to do before he went to bed. He opened his laptop and connected to Zoom. A figure appeared, a uniformed man.

"Treasurer, thank you for meeting me so late. I just want to thank you for stepping in and ensuring the investigation into the attack on Melanie Chambers got buried. We don't need well-meaning officers, snooping around and digging up things they shouldn't. I am sure Melanie Chambers will do the right thing." He sipped from his whisky glass.

"A pleasure Chairman, may I also say what a masterstroke it was with the attack on Suzanne Frost, an ingenious way to stir up hatred. You will also be pleased to know that I now have a small team of officers willing to act on our behalf. Several are highly skilled in 'dark arts.'" The Treasurer smiled and light reflected off the pips on his epaulettes, giving him the aura of a Hollywood hero of some kind. The Chairman bade him good night and closed the meeting. Just then his phone buzzed and a message popped up. He opened it and saw a selfie of the Secretary lying naked on a bed, *"Missing you xx"* was the comment. Another message from her popped up. He read it. *She is good, this woman, very good.*

At the same time as The Chairman was receiving explicit sexual images of The Secretary, Johnny Saint lay in bed in his room in the hotel just off Eastbourne Seafront. It was not just that it was noisy from revellers under the influence of drink or drugs but he was also troubled. He had seen someone earlier in the day, whilst being in the crowd at the funeral of Suzanne Frost. Someone he had not expected to see. At the time he had been wondering why it was that so many people grieved for someone they did not know. Was it the manner of their death? Was it a sense of community pain? Was it a lack of understanding of the eternal nature of the soul? In his mind, he knew that the soul was immortal, that faith in Jesus brought your soul into his presence at death. That on the Last Day your soul and body would reunite and Christ himself would judge all humanity. Those who did not believe were to be cast into the lake of fire for an eternity of separation from the love and peace of Christ, a second death. It broke his heart to think that so many people refused to acknowledge Jesus as Lord and their future was not a bright one.

As he had stood pondering all this in the autumn sunshine outside St Mary's Church in Hamstead, his eyes had locked on to one of the mourners. A man in his early forties, smartly dressed and with a pretty woman of similar age. As he stared at the man for a second he recognised him. Such was the shock that for a moment he froze. It seemed that the man had recognised him too. This was not good news. He had tried hard to isolate himself from previous lives and cut all ties when he moved on to begin again. Up to now, he had been successful. He had never bumped into old friends. He had recovered quickly, slipped away into the crowd, and found a quiet coffee shop in which to think.

Back in his hotel room, in the dark, he prayed. As he did so, a sense of peace enveloped him and he allowed the Spirit to direct his thoughts. He remembered the young boy, the church youth group, and the angry boy who hated God. It came flooding back. The more he remembered the more he felt his Lord speak. *Go to him. Sam needs you.*

THIRTY

Melanie Chambers' flat in Wimbledon was a mess. Not only had the intruder daubed red paint on the wall in the main lounge but they had emptied the desk and filing drawers and even turned out all Melanie's clothes in the bedroom. She stood in the lounge and began to sob, again.

"Hey, it's okay we're here. We will help." Sally put her arms around her and held her tight. Sam was on the phone to a cleaning and decorating company. His ability to pay over the top meant someone was coming the same day to clean and begin the task of completely redecorating the whole flat.

"Let's start sorting the clothes in your bedroom; we can wash them all if you like?" Sally was keen to distract Mel from lingering on the horrific events of recent days. There was a knock at the door that made Mel jump.

"I've got it," said Sam soothingly. "Don't worry." Sally took Mel into the bedroom and Sam could hear them chatting away beginning to sort out the clothes. He opened the main door after using the spy hole to check who it was. A uniformed police officer waited outside. He opened the door.

"Ms Chambers? Is she here?" The officer was a woman in her early thirties, with black hair tied neatly back in a bun that made her look stern, like an old-fashioned image of a strict school teacher.

"Yes, come in. I am Sam Tucker, a friend. We are here to help her sort out the mess." The officer smiled and stepped into the flat.

"That's good of you. I have a progress report on the burglary and assault. I need to speak to Ms Chambers." At that moment, Mel and Sally emerged from the bedroom with a bundle of clothes each, ready for the washing machine.

"With you in a minute, officer." Sally led Mel into the kitchen and they both quickly returned having deposited the washing on the floor by the washing machine.

The police officer sat on the edge of the sofa, looking uncomfortable at the words she was about to speak.

Mel sat opposite in a comfy chair and Sally and Sam stood behind her, like guardian angels.

"Firstly may I say how sorry I am that you experienced this trauma." She opened her notebook to ensure she didn't miss anything. "The forensic team did not recover any DNA evidence other than your own from the lounge or bedroom. It appears that he wore nitrile gloves, similar to any available in most chemists. The small fibres recovered from under your nails were from a sweatshirt and this also is common to many brands. None of your neighbours have come forward with any information. House-to-house questioning had led to nothing either. The red paint was a brand available in all DIY stores up until ten years ago. It was old and the paint had partly gone off. Therefore, it would be difficult to trace. I am afraid it is not good news." She closed the notebook.

"So what now? Said Melanie somewhat forlornly.

"The case will remain open, but no further investigation will take place unless new evidence comes to light. I am sorry." She stood and began to leave.

"So that's it? Just like that, nothing else?" Sam was fuming. Sally placed a hand on his arm.

"Sam, it's not her fault. She is just the messenger."

"But…"

"It's okay Sam. I'll be fine. The locks are being changed and you've kindly organised the redecorating. You've been so kind."

The police officer said her goodbyes and left. Sam shut the door firmly behind her. She moved off towards the lifts and as she did so sent a text addressed to *The Treasurer*.

Case closed, no more concerns.

"Mel, come and stay with us for a few days. We can show you around the farm. Just whilst the flat is redone. Please." Sally was insistent and pleading at the same time.

"Okay, I have to work for a couple of days but I promise I'll come down at the weekend." Mel smiled appreciatively. "Thank you."

THIRTY-ONE

Johnny Saint drove his newly acquired red Honda 50cc scooter down the farm track towards what appeared to be a shop with a barn, a carpark and offices above. Several cars were parked and the shop looked busy. He parked his scooter, removed his helmet and left it on the seat of the scooter. From his pocket, he took his phone and opened the Facebook page for Downs Wood Farm. He re-read the advert.

Estate assistant required

35 hours a week, flexible and some unsocial hours. Accommodation provided.

Main duties, supporting the Estate manager in tending to crops, working in the farm shop, some gardening and in the long-term site management of a campsite.

Initial salary 22K. improving when the campsite opens.

The rest of the advert was the contact details and address. He had contacted a man called Ian and arranged an interview. It hadn't taken him long to discover this was where Sam lived after understanding that Sam needed him. The advert had popped up in a timely way as he had pondered how to make contact with Sam and why Sam would need him. *God does work in mysterious ways; I know that for sure.*

Ian had been impressed with John's experience as they spoke over the phone and invited him straight up. To be honest, he wasn't sure why he needed an assistant but Sam had mentioned it as a way of supporting both himself and Kelly. "Another pair of hands" he had said, and if this bloke Johnny was anything to go by then he would fit the bill.

"So tell me a bit about your time as a fisherman, Johnny. I am intrigued; the owner has plans to create a fishing lake."

"It was a large lake in a warmer climate, a long time ago." They wandered the estate, Ian explaining how things worked and Johnny listening intently and asking questions. Johnny shared his many different experiences as a fisherman, farmer, aid worker, soldier, and medic. He told of his love of the outdoors and his spiritual stance as a Christian. Ian wasn't too fussed by that as long as he was a good worker. Ian spent some time trying to gauge the man's age. He was clearly fit and healthy, with a strong physique, but he must be in his mid-sixties. He certainly didn't have any issues when he walked the estate, no breathlessness or complaining of being old. Maybe he'd be okay. He showed Johnny the accommodation above the farm shop. There were two estate offices with a small kitchenette and bathroom. There was also a one-bedroom flat with a lounge, kitchen and bathroom. It was fully furnished in a modern style and looked fresh and unused.

"This part of the barn is a new addition, we had it made to blend in. We use the estate offices but the flat has never been used. I am prepared to give you a three-month trial, off the record, cash in hand, then if you like us and we like you we can make it permanent." Ian held out a hand to confirm the deal and Johnny took it. "You can move in today if you like and start on Monday, give yourself time to acclimatise." Johnny shook his hand enthusiastically.

"Thank you, Ian, you're a gentleman. I'm looking forward to meeting the boss and the rest of the family. I feel at home here already. Ronnie the dog raced up to them and Johnny knelt down and held out a hand. Ronnie placed a paw in it, wagged his tail and barked a welcome.

"Blimey," said Ian, scratching his head, "he's normally not that friendly. You must be pretty special."

THIRTY-TWO

Christos had arrived in London, with not only Maria and Thomas but fully prepared for a major surveillance operation. He deposited his wife and child in their small hotel in Wimbledon before heading straight off to Melanie Chambers' flat. From his vantage point in a small coffee shop, he could see the front door of the modern purpose-built block of flats. There were no curtains in the first-floor flat, a fact that helped him see that the decorators were packing up for the day. He could see Melanie talking to one of them. She was gesticulating with both arms. He had been told one arm was in a sling. He checked the photo on his phone. It was definitely Melanie Chambers he could see. *Maybe it got better?* He sipped a double espresso and munched on a ham and cheese panini. It was going to be a long night. He had been told that Mel was off to work tonight and would travel down to Sam and Sally's on Friday. He had two days of solid surveillance. *Maybe I'm getting too old for this.*

An hour after the decorators left just as dusk began to settle on the land. Melanie Chambers emerged from the block of flats. She was dressed for a night out or a date. Christos casually used his phone to take photos. She was wearing a black glitzy dress that sparkled in the fading sunlight as she walked. He noticed that her stockings or tights had a slight lacy pattern on them and her shoes were heeled and open-toed. She had a small handbag slung across one shoulder and carried a lightweight jacket on her arm. Her make-up was well done and tasteful to enhance her beauty. *This woman is not on her way to work.* He quickly finished his third espresso, left twenty pounds under the cup and left taking his rucksack of equipment with him. He followed at a distance noticing that there was no bandage on her arm as he had expected and her arm moved freely without pain. He followed her into Wimbledon station and down onto the platform. She stepped onto the District Line tube heading for Upminster. She changed at South Kensington made her way to Green Park and then Euston. The final leg of her journey took her into the heart of North London. Christos took care to keep out of sight, always a fair distance behind, perhaps sat in an adjacent carriage, ensuring that she never caught sight of him. He was able to casually photograph her and also scan the other passengers for any signs she was being followed. There was none.

Melanie Chambers emerged from the tube station and into the night air. She slipped on her jacket, it was cooler than she had expected. She walked along the busy street that gave Christos excellent cover; he kept her in sight about thirty yards behind her. After several minutes she turned into what appeared to be an exclusive housing estate. He watched from the corner as she approached a large detached house. He removed his long-lensed Nikon camera, specially designed for night photography and began snapping images, ensuring he caught the house number and Melanie waiting at the front door. The door opened and he got a perfect shot of a tall blonde man. They kissed. Click, another image captured. Christos replaced the camera into his bag and walked casually around the estate towards the house. There were security cameras at the front, he assumed at the rear too. However, the next door house had none and was in darkness. He walked down the path and around to the side gate. Finding it unlocked he quietly slipped down the path into the rear of the property. Sticking to the shadows, he snuck across the patio and looked over the fence. He could see the camera of the house next door, guarding the front and one directed across the patio to the French doors at the rear. As he watched, a cat walked across in front of the French doors and sat about three feet out from the house. The emergency lighting remained off. Christos bent down picked up a piece of gravel and flicked it towards the cat. It jumped and sprinted out down the garden. The lights came on. Christos could see there was a blind spot right up close to the house that the camera did not cover. *Poor design, good for me.*

Just then, the French doors opened and the man emerged. From the shadow of next door, Christos watched him. "It is just next door's cat."

"Leave the doors darling, it's so hot in here, I feel like I want to strip off!" The tall blonde man smiled, the smile of a man who had all he wanted at this very moment in time. He turned and went back inside. Christos waited for the security light to go off and then carefully climbed over the fence into the darkened side ally of the house. Keeping his back to the wall of the house he edged around towards the French doors. He was in a dangerous position, if they came out again he would be caught. He carefully pulled a tiny but powerful microphone and recorder, no bigger than a five-pence piece and crouched down. He peeled a protective cover revealing the sticky glue and carefully placed it on the glass of the door, right in the corner, almost unnoticeable, especially as there were long flowery curtains at the edge of the door. He retreated and climbed back over the fence into the next-door garden.

Christos made his way to the bottom of the garden towards the shed adjacent to the garden of the house where Melanie Chambers was. Melanie and the blonde man were still in the lounge, the lights were on and the curtains and the door were still open. *Lucky for me,* thought Christos as he clambered onto the shed roof, lay flat in the darkness and retrieved his Nikon once again. He also plugged in his earpiece and set the recorder going from his phone. As he listened to their conversation he snapped away at the couple who sat eating and drinking. Before long Christos realised they were more than friends. He stopped taking photos before they became too pornographic, but it was clear that Melanie and this man were lovers.

Christos retraced his steps and retrieved his microphone. It was after midnight and it seemed that Melanie and the man were in bed. He had seen the upstairs lights go on and both Melanie and the man, naked and embracing at the window. He assumed they were in for the night. As he walked back to the tube station, he uploaded the images and recording to the server in Sam's office into a file called 'Christos.'

THIRTY-THREE

"You did what?" Sam couldn't believe what Christos had done. "I wasn't expecting surveillance like that. Just follow her around. I don't need to know her private life." Christos winced as Sam told him off down the phone. In the background he could hear Sally, trying to calm him down and also asking "What was he like? Where do they live? Why didn't she mention a boyfriend to us? Why didn't he help when her flat got burgled?"

"Sorry, I got carried away. I've uploaded it all to the server. It sounded like a business dinner with a special dessert!" He smirked at his own smuttiness. It made Sam smile too and realise, it wasn't a disaster as no one got hurt.

"A business dinner, you say?" Both Sam and Sally sounded intrigued.

"Yeah, they kept talking about a series of events, I think and how successful they were. They even spoke about similar events abroad and other teams working with them. They even had teams in the US and the Middle East. I think it was some kind of charity work."

"I didn't know she was involved in charity?" Said Sam in a puzzled way.

"You hardly know the woman Sam; why would you know?" Sally's tone showed how stupid she thought he was for making such a comment.

"Anyway, it's all on the server, if you ever want to look at it. Sorry again. I'll stick to shadowing her." He'd failed to mention that he had returned to her flat in the small hours, picked the new locks, and searched her flat. He planted another tiny recorder under her bedside table and one under the coffee table. There was a mobile on the kitchen table, he hacked it and downloaded the contacts and messages. He knew it would be there as part of the conversation he had recorded mentioned the fact she had left her mobile at home. The man had been concerned and for a moment, there had been sharp words. This had raised alarm bells in Christos' head. There was something about the man that worried him, he was vaguely familiar. It wasn't until he was on the tube to Wimbledon that he realised who it was. He decided further investigation was necessary before he spoke to Sam and Sally. He would just have to do this on his own. Old school style!

Johnny Saint unloaded his bag from the boot of the taxi and hauled it up to his new flat. It had been a small logistical puzzle to get both his scooter, his luggage and himself all over to Downs Wood Farm, but he had done it. He unpacked what luggage he had and settled himself down on the sofa with a cup of sweet tea. He loved to spend time alone, quietly reflecting and praying. He used the time to recharge and remember that he was never alone. A knock at the door brought him back into the present.

"It's open, come straight in," he called loudly. He stood up ready to greet whoever wanted to see him. Sam stepped into the room and held out his hand to greet his new employee.

"Hi, I'm Sam Tu..." He stopped in mid-sentence. Then began again. "It's you. From the funeral. I thought I knew you..." His mind was buzzing, trying to figure out where he knew this man from. Johnny stepped around from the sofa and held out his hand for Sam to shake.

"I'm Johnny, I'm your new estate assistant."

"Have we met before, Johnny?" Sam was convinced they had, but couldn't place it. His eyes were familiar. Even his voice.

Johnny repeated himself; "I'm Johnny." This time with more emphasis on his name. They shook hands.

"Johnny? Johnny?" Sam kept repeating it to help him remember. Then as if a veil had been lifted from his mind. "Not Johnny from Church in London. You can't be, that would make you about a hundred years old!" Sam laughed at the thought. "That was twenty-five years ago! No, I must be wrong." Johnny smiled a big toothy smile and his eyes sparkled.

"Fu…" Sam quickly held his hand over his mouth. "Shit! You are him aren't you?"

Johnny nodded and kept smiling, giving Sam time to process the information.

"I thought you were old back then, maybe I was just a kid and misjudged your age!"

"Possibly," said Johnny and opened his arms for a proper greeting.

"It's good to see you Sam, you seem to have done well for yourself." He embraced Sam lovingly. They parted and Sam stepped back. You don't look a day over sixty-five. You must live a healthy life! I thought you were mid-sixties twenty-five years ago."

"I keep fit, I walk a lot, and God has blessed me with health!" Johnny sat down and motioned Sam to sit too.

"You still into all the God stuff, then? I'm still wavering. But recent events are making me question."

"Yeah, I'm still into it. I'd like to hear about your experiences and the questions you have." He nodded sagely.

For the next hour, they sat and talked, drank tea and caught up. Sam explained how he became wealthy and talked about his wife and business. Johnny listened and chipped in with a few adventures of his own.

"When I left London so suddenly, one of my brothers abroad needed help. I had to travel quickly. I'm sorry I never got to say goodbye." Johnny was careful in how he phrased everything, he did not want to lie but also did not want to reveal too much about himself.

"You must meet Sally. I assume you know Ian and Kelly." Johnny nodded. *This was going to be more challenging than he had thought. Why was he here, why does Sam need me? God does certainly send me on some strange missions.*

"Come to dinner tonight, we have a houseful arriving. Bad planning really but it will be fun!" Sam was so excited at the arrival of an old mentor and friend that he did not consider anything other going on but that which he took at face value.

THIRTY-FOUR

Melanie Chambers arrived at Downs Wood Farm in mid-afternoon. The late September sunshine was pleasant but there was a breeze coming in off the sea and she shivered as she unloaded a small cabin bag. Ronnie ran up to her, barking and wagging his tail.

"Enough of that Ronnie!" called Sally as she emerged from the farmhouse. She sauntered over to Melanie who was busy petting Ronnie who had flirted outrageously with her.

"Leave Mel alone, she doesn't want you flirting like a dirty old man." She shooed the dog away. But he persisted in circling them, his tail wagging and giving the occasional welcome bark.

Sally hugged her and took her bag. "It is so good to see you. How are the redecorations going? How is your arm?" She led her towards the farmhouse.

"It's all good thanks. I'm slowly getting over the shock." She held her arm where the bandage was. "Kelly is inside, you'll love her. We'll show you around the estate and what we're doing." Sally was quite excited to have a celebrity as a friend and that she was staying in her home.

Christos and the family arrived an hour later in a rental car. Sam and Ian replaced the women as hosts and helped them settle in. Further tours of Downs Wood Farm took place before everyone settled down to dinner in the dining room that had a stunning view down a valley towards the sea. Much of the valley belonged to the farm but it was rented as pasture to generate income and keep the land in use.

Dinner was three courses; a mezze of Greek salads and small bites with pitta bread and yoghurt dips. This was followed by slow-roasted shanks of lamb with a tomato and herb sauce on a bed of rice. They finished off with Baklava, a cheese board, liqueurs and coffee. The atmosphere seemed light, relaxed and friendly. People getting to know each other. Melanie Chambers was the most animated, wanting to know everything about everyone in the room, and asking questions that elicited some interesting responses. People seemed to open up to her. She was an excellent journalist and interviewer.

"So, Johnny, tell me how you know Sam? What brings you to Sussex at this particular time?" Melanie leaned forward across the table, a big smile on her face, picked a grape from the cheese board and popped it in her mouth.

Johnny had been relatively quiet, enjoying listening to the lives of others; he was always reticent to share his own story. For one, there was far too much to tell and mainly because he always gave the impression that no one would be particularly interested in him.

"Well," he said, mirroring Melanie's actions and popping some cheese in his mouth. "Some years ago, when Sam was a teenager, I was his youth worker for a while. We got to know each other quite well. Since then I've been abroad on various projects. I recently returned and saw this job, here. I thought it would be a good place to begin to slow down a little, maybe retire into obscurity." He tried to be vague, realising how much detail Melanie had already gleaned from Christos and Sam.

"And what is it you did abroad, what kind of projects?" Melanie smiled an innocent smile but Johnny noticed the steel in her eyes.

"I was an aid worker for various people, churches, and organisations." He hoped this would be enough to satisfy her. It was not.

"What kind of aid? Disaster relief or longer-term projects? Which charities? It would be interesting to find out, perhaps I could do a documentary about you Johnny? You seem to have a lifetime or more of experience."

Careful, this woman is prying. This is more than just a casual chat. The thought formed in Johnny's mind and he was aware of his senses warning him that something was not right with this woman.

"I'm just a man in the background, who wants to help others. There is nothing special about me. Don't waste your film on me. Sam here has a much more interesting story, or Christos and Maria. A taverna on Patmos, what could be more romantic than that?" He tried hard to make his tone light and friendly and deflect Melanie Chambers from questioning him more. He gestured with his hand toward Christos and Maria. They grinned.

"It's not that glamourous, it is hard work." Maria chipped in.

"Anyway, Christos had an interesting life before he met me! Tell her about being a secret agent." Maria nudged her husband playfully.

"Now that does sound interesting, tell me more" Melanie's attention turned from Johnny and her focus became fixed on Christos, who was happy to recount vaguely accurate stories of his escapades in the Greek secret service. Melanie lapped it up, asking more and more questions.

Johnny sat back, relieved. Sam noticed him and noted his slight anxiety. He filed it away for later.

As Christos recounted his life in the Secret Service, they moved into the lounge and made themselves comfortable. There was much laughter and it seemed like new friendships were being formed. Johnny stood up from his seat and began to clear away plates and glasses, and Sam helped him, wanting time with his old friend alone. As they loaded the dishwasher, the conversation turned to Sam's book and his interest in the apostle John.

"So why John? What is so fascinating about him?" Johnny seemed genuinely interested in Sam's current obsession.

"To be honest, I was asked to write about him, based on the success of the one I did on myths and legends. It was just a hobby, but it seems to have taken off." Sam loaded the last of the plates into the washer and turned it on.

"So, you think that John, the disciples and even Jesus were just legends?" Johnny was genuinely surprised.

"Oh no, they were real all right. Genuine people. The evidence is overwhelming. It is just the legends surrounding John that interest me."

"Legends?" Johnny looked puzzled. Sam turned to him with a look of surprise on his face.

"Surely, you must know of the legends of St John. Immortal, unable to die until Christ returns. There are stories and sightings of the apostle John throughout Christian history. The breathing grave, the helper to Muslims in the Crusades, the mysterious preacher who persuaded Queen Elizabeth the First to end the persecution of Catholics and give freedom of worship. There are so many!" Sam was becoming enthused. Johnny just shrugged and pulled a face that suggested ignorance.

"But aren't these just myths? You don't really think he is alive now, two thousand years later. That's crazy, Sam." Johnny sauntered back into the dining room to finish clearing away the detritus of the meal. Sam followed him. They could hear the conversations and laughter coming from the lounge, but it was quiet where they were.

"I didn't when I began, but things have changed. I am beginning to wonder if it is true."

"Why? What has changed your mind?" Johnny was curious. With a deep breath, Sam began to tell the story of the summer and their meeting with Father Luca in the Vatican, The Six, their trip to Patmos, meeting Christos, their time in Israel, the murders and attacks and the shootings in Germany. By the time he had finished, they were sitting at the kitchen table with coffees.

"I even had Christos follow Melanie after the burglary to make sure she was safe." Sam sat back and took a big sip of his coffee. He waited for Johnny's response.

Johnny sat for a moment, weighing up his response. Sam had presented a compelling case but he needed to reflect carefully on it. He cupped his hands around his mug of coffee and began to speak.

"That's a powerful story, Sam. One that has a ring of truth. There are too many coincidences. Your research appears sound. That software you have seems amazing. So many people called John throughout history all doing good works in the name of Jesus. Could they all be the same person? Why are they not just different people called John?" He tried to sound balanced, he did not want to quash his friend's enthusiasm.

"Ah, as you said, Johnny, too many coincidences. Also, there is a pattern to all the stories I have uncovered."

"A pattern?" Johnny gave a quizzical look.

"Yeah, in every account the mysterious 'John' just arrives in a place or situation, like the stranger in a "Fistful of Dollars", or Jack Reacher in those novels by Lee Child. He sorts out a problem or helps for a while and then disappears off the scene. Just vanishes. There is never any trace of death, with any of them!"

Johnny was about to speak when the party began to break up. Sam looked up at the kitchen clock; it was just after midnight. Sally, Kelly and Mel wandered back into the kitchen all slightly worse for wear with drink. Ian was outside locking up all the outbuildings and Christos and Maria had already gone to bed.

"Let's carry this on tomorrow, Sam. I am fascinated by your work." Johnny stood up and made his way to the door.

"Hey, don't leave, not before giving me a kiss." Melanie wobbled over to Johnny and slung her arms around his heck. She tried to kiss him on the lips but he turned his head just in time. She planted a kiss on his cheek. "Oh well, I tried," she said in a slightly slurred way.

There were hugs around and eventually, the kitchen emptied. Johnny crossed the yard to the entrance to the shop where his first-floor apartment was situated, moonlight guiding him. He shivered in the cool night air. He had a lot to think about. It was going to be a long night of prayer and reflection, but he was beginning to understand why he was here. *Clint Eastwood, I like that.*

THIRTY-FIVE

Sam stood by the kitchen window and watched Sally, Melanie and Maria casually chatting as they walked across the yard from the farm shop. It was a blustery autumn morning, clouds moving swiftly across the sky creating a display of shapes and patterns. The wind played with their hair causing them to sweep it from their eyes. They had been to get bread and milk. It was a boon having the shop on your property. Sam had made breakfast, and the smell of bacon, eggs and toast wafted through the house, enticing people to eat and testing their resolve to eat healthily. He was waiting for them to return. Christos was playing 'Jenga' with his son in the lounge; he could hear the laughter and crash of the wooden bricks. His eyes were drawn to a figure walking back down the path towards the shop. It was Johnny, Ronnie was with him scampering ahead and snuffling around in the grass and bushes that lined the path. As he thought about Johnny suddenly arriving back in his life all these years after he had just vanished when he was a teenager, the mist began to clear in his mind. *Johnny fits the pattern of the apostle.* It shook him to the core. He had been so blind, so excited to see his old friend that the thought had never occurred to him.

"Of course! It all fits." He said aloud to no one. Just then, the door opened and the three women walked in. Sally carried two fresh loaves of sourdough and Mel carried the milk. Sam shook his head to clear the thought. He needed time to process this. *I could be jumping to a massively wrong conclusion*, he thought.

"Sam, we've been talking outside," Mel gestured towards the other women. "Now that I am over the shock of the burglary, we need to talk more about The Six and your research on John. What else do you have? I am not going to let some thug stop me from finding the truth." Mel set the milk on the table and almost summoned Sam to sit next to her around the large oak table in the kitchen. "Tell me, what do you know? Does John really exist? If so, where is he? We need to protect him from the 'Six.'" Sam glared at Sally, uncomfortable at Mel's forthright approach. If his thoughts about Johnny were true, he needed to be careful about sharing information.

They sat down to a breakfast of bacon, eggs, fried tomatoes and sourdough toast, tea, coffee and fruit juice. Sam tried to deflect the discussion, but Melanie was forcing the issue.

"Have you discovered anymore since the burglary? Does John really exist? Do you know any more about The Six?" She was pressing him hard, even Sally and Christos noticed the aggression in her voice.

"Mel, I've told you everything I know at the moment. If John is real, he could be anywhere on the planet. If The Six, whoever they are, think he is real, well good luck in finding him. He has evaded capture and death for two thousand years. I can't see that a bunch of crazy atheists are going to get him." Mel bristled at the comment.

"What do you mean crazy?"

"Well," said Sam, "I don't call killing a bunch of pensioners in Israel or shooting churchgoers in Germany, rational do you?"

"You can't judge people just because they have a different opinion, Sam." Mel clicked into journalist mode.

"I am all for religious freedom and the freedom not to believe, but I am against terrorists who are trying to control others with fear and violence. Whether they are religious or atheist!" He could feel himself becoming agitated by the discussion. His heart rate increased and a tightening in his stomach developed.

Christos chipped in as best he could with a mouthful of bacon sandwich. "Mel, it sounds like you're sympathetic to The Sixs' cause." He was joking but it backfired.

"What do you mean; you think I am a terrorist? How dare you! I was burgled and assaulted by them. You arrogant..." She leaned over the table and took a swing at Christos. Sally grabbed her arm and pulled her back.

"Not in my house!" boomed Sally, and Mel slumped back into the chair. She covered her face with her hands and began to sob. Her shoulders shook as the tears flowed.

"Sor… sorr… sorry Sally. I don't know what came over me?" Her voice faltered over the words.

"I guess I am not over it." She cried, letting all the tension go. The room went quiet. Maria took Thomas away to get him dressed. Sam scurried around clearing the table and Christos sat and observed quietly. Sally placed a loving arm around her new friend and walked her through to the lounge.

In the now empty kitchen, Christos spoke. "Sam, I am sorry but I needed to provoke her."

Sam turned to face him. Confusion all over his face.

"What? Why would you do that?" He could feel the tension rise again in his body. He stepped over to where Christos sat and sat opposite him. "Why?"

"Did you notice her arm when Sally grabbed it?" He motioned with his head to the place where the recent unpleasantness took place. Sam automatically turned his head, despite the room being empty.

"What? What should I have seen?"

"She did not flinch or register pain. That was the arm that was in a sling and scarred by the assailant in her apartment. It is less than a week. Has it healed completely?" Christos let the question hang and allowed Sam to draw conclusions. After what seemed like an age, Sam spoke.

"Are you saying she's lying and her arm wasn't hurt? But I saw her in a sling. We both did." Sam was struggling with this new train of thought.

"Did you see the injury or just a bandage?" Sam thought for a moment. Christos could almost see him processing his thoughts.

"Just a bandage but... the flat, it was a mess, she was distraught, the message, the paint on the wall."

"It's all a lie." Christos fished his mobile from his pocket and scrolled through his pictures. He passed it across to Sam. Sam looked and his eyes widened. It showed an image of Melanie Chambers in a glitzy short dress with patterned stockings and a jacket slung over one shoulder. Her arms were bare; there was no bandage. Further, more close-up, photos showed no injury on her arm. "This was last week when I arrived in London, two days after the incident." Sam stood up and was about to go into the lounge, his anger roused.

"Wait, my friend. There is much more. I did a little more snooping over the past few days. I recognised the man she met when I followed her. I was concerned about some of the things he said. So I broke into Melanie's apartment."

Sam almost burst. "What?"

"It's okay," Christos, gestured with his hands. "No one will ever know I have been there."

Sam relaxed slightly, but a sense of being out of control began to creep towards him like water oozing across the floor and trapping him the corner.

"I cloned her phone, planted a couple of receivers and searched the place. Including the garage block, where I found..."

"Red paint?" Sam chipped in. Christos nodded.

"What is she playing at? Some crazy game?" Sam was totally bemused and angry at being taken for a ride.

"You need to get rid of her for a couple of days. Look at the stuff I uploaded. I don't think she is as innocent as she makes out. Then make a plan." Christos was taking control, his intelligence training kicking in.

"Sally is going to want to kill her when she finds out. She'll be fuming." In the miasma caused by Melanie's lies, Sam totally forgot about the revelation about his friend John.

THIRTY-SIX

"I don't believe it, I don't believe it!" Sam kept repeating the phrase every time Christos showed him photos and he listened to recordings Christos had made during his surveillance of Melanie Chambers. There was so much he did not understand. He looked at the picture of Melanie and the blonde man and his jaw dropped.

"Robert Frost! Mel and Robert. But his wife has just died. We went to the funeral." Sam was flabbergasted.

"It appears they have been seeing each other for a while. The conversations were not those of new lovers but of people comfortable with each other. This was not their first liaison."

Sam had suggested that Sally take Mel, Maria, and Thomas to Brighton for the day. He needed Mel out of the way. Now he and Christos sat in Sam's office. The multiple screens revealed more of Melanie Chambers' secrets.

"There are five obscure contacts. Titles not names." He scrolled through the screenshots of Mel's phone contacts that he had taken from her cloned phone. "Chairman, this appears to be Frost, by the nature of the messages, some very explicit. Then there is HR, PR, Treasurer and Administrator. I suppose they could be linked to the charity work I recorded them talking about. It is worth checking." Christos looked hopefully at Sam, waiting for the instruction to go ahead and use his former skills once again.

"Five, eh? With Mel, that makes six. Six!" he repeated the number for emphasis.

"Hang on Sam; let's get the facts straight first. Yes, Mel lied about her injury and the burglary. I don't know why. Yes, she is having an affair she kept secret. That's none of our business. You cannot assume she is a terrorist. Look at all the evidence I collected first." Christos was the voice of reason, although he knew more than Sam did and had already drawn his own conclusions; Sam needed to see it for himself.

"Evidence? What have you been up to? You were only supposed to follow Mel for a few days."

"I know, but I did a bit of digging around and used my old contacts in the UK. Each of these obscure numbers is a trustee of a charity called *Digamma.* They are a scientific trust, promoting rational or scientific learning and secular values. They are a legitimate cause registered with the charity commission. They fundraise and do events globally to promote a rational and logical way of life." Christos clicked on their website. It looked legitimate enough. In the top corner was their logo, a version of the traditional symbol for an atom. The nucleus surrounded by six electrons. The word Digamma underneath in a dynamic and aggressive font. Sam read the vision statement aloud.

"Digamma, creating a rational and logical world. Promoting learning, peace and freedom." He continued scanning the website, looking at the events and conferences that they had put on. The calendar for the next year was full. Events globally with branches of Digamma in the Americas, Australia, Asia and the Middle East. He clicked on the trustee's page and saw photos of six well-known people. Two of whom he knew personally. Robert Frost was named as the Chairman of the Charity for Europe and Melanie Chambers was listed as the Company secretary. The others were a high-ranking Metropolitan Police officer, the CEO of a large retail company, a celebrity medal-winning UK athlete and an elderly female actor. Sam sat back and looked at Christos.

"It looks legitimate and it matches up with the conversations you recorded at Frost's house. However, you are right it doesn't make Mel a terrorist." Sam was a little disappointed. "But why would she fake a burglary and injury?" Christos tapped the keyboard and the screen changed.

"I took the liberty of asking an old MI5 friend to search for anything linked to the symbol of the charity. He came up with this on the dark web. Sam began to read, and as he did so, his eyes widened.

"New Atomists?"

"Yes, an atheistic movement across the world based on ancient Greek philosophy that everything is logical and scientific. Religion is false and needs to be eradicated like cancer needs to be removed from a body. They are hedonistic, amoral and ruthless."

"Are you saying The Six are new atomists? It makes sense; they fit the profile. This is way too big for us. Give everything to your MI5 mate. Let them deal with it." Sam was shaking his head. Christos changed the screen again back to the charity website.

"Look, the symbol is the same, it even has six electrons. I am Greek, and the word Digamma is a Greek word. It is the number six. This is a front for The Six, so they have a legitimate reason to be in contact, and have each other's numbers. It is the perfect cover. No one would suspect them. They are pillars of the community, well respected. Melanie is a terrorist and so is Robert Frost. They are on a quest to eradicate religious belief and create an elitist, hedonistic society where pleasure reigns above compassion and justice." Christos sat back and looked at his friend.

Sam said nothing; his mind was in shock. It took him several minutes to process all that he had heard. A movement out in the yard caught his eye as he stared out of his office window. It was Johnny. He was wheeling a barrow of freshly dug potatoes to the shop. As usual, Ronnie was with him, scampering around.

"John," he said suddenly. "They are after John; if they find him and kill him it will disprove the Christian faith."

"We don't know where he is, or even IF he is. They will never find him even if he exists." Christos was confident in the way he spoke. Sam just pointed out of the window. "John!"

They sat in John's apartment over the farm shop. Johnny made coffee and placed some pastries on the table. Christos picked one up and bit into it. A piece of apple nearly escaped but he caught it with his tongue. Sam was a little agitated. Since remembering his revelation about his friend, he was keen to know if his assertions were true.

"Johnny, can I ask you something?" Sam's tone was solemn.

"Sounds serious," Johnny replied, trying to lighten the mood, but he knew why Sam was there. *He has to discover it himself. He has to know the truth. This is why I am here.*

"Johnny, I know this will sound crazy, but I promise you, I am not mad. You know that I have an interest in mythology and Biblical history. You will know, of course, the story in John twenty-one, which leads to the legend that the apostle John is immortal and cannot die until Christ returns."

Johnny nodded. "Of course, but isn't that just a legend?" He smiled knowingly. "Do you think I am him? You think I am John the apostle."

"Are you?"

"What makes you think so?" Christos munched on a second pastry and listened quietly.

Sam proceeded to remind him of the patterns that he had discovered in all the legend stories,

"Remember, Clint Eastwood, Jack Reacher. You fit the bill, Johnny. That's you."

"I see," he said. "So I am Clint Eastwood?" he laughed but then became serious. "Look I am no hero; I am a nobody, just someone who wants to help others."

"Exactly, Johnny, you're a Christian, you live under the radar, you help others; you go from place to place, never settling for too long anywhere. You are Johan, Johannes, John the preacher,

Jan the mysterious medic, and Hans the rescuer of Jews from Germany and many more I suspect. I've researched them all. I found a letter in a local war museum in Newhaven that told your story. Tom Brennan, Remember him?"

Johnny sat very still. Then in a measured voice, full of gentleness he spoke. "If I was John the apostle, what difference would it make to you? Would it change you? And you Christos, would it change you, knowing that I am John?" Both men were silent for a moment.

"If you are him, Johnny, then you are in danger. There are people who want you dead. People who want to rid the world of people like you, believers, and people of faith. They want a selfish, self-centred world for the rich to live as they please. You pose a threat because you stand for everything they hate. Killing you would undermine the whole of the Christian faith." Sam spoke passionately, clearly angry at the thought of good people dying so that others could enjoy their own lives as they wished. Johnny raised an eyebrow; it made him look a little like Roger Moore.

"How do you know this Sam? This seems very far-fetched. If I were John the Apostle then I hardly think someone would come looking here for me." He tried to sound nonchalant but deep inside him his spirit stirred. *Listen to him, he's trustworthy, he is trying to protect you.*

"A lovely Italian priest told me, Father Luca, I think you met him many years ago. He's dead now. The Six, this organisation bent on destroying faith, had him killed in their attempt to find you!" Sam pointed at Johnny in an almost accusatory way. At the mention of Luca's name, Johnny's eyes flickered with recognition. It didn't go unnoticed by Sam and Christos.

"The Six? The number of earthly things, Satan's number. That's interesting. That number has represented evil throughout history, just as seven represents completeness and fullness. Six equates with brokenness and dissatisfaction."

Sam took a risk, "Johnny, what do you know about the Apostel–Johannes–Geimeindezentrum or the John the Apostle Centre in Berlin?"

"Why do you ask?" A look of concern flicked across his eyes.

"The Six massacred the congregation as they came out of church last week, shortly after one of their volunteer workers, a Johan Heiliger or John Saint disappeared." Johnny bowed his head, his shoulders sagged and he began to weep. Sam pressed on needing to know the truth.

"Johnny, was that you in Berlin? Are you Johan Heiliger? What is your surname? I can ask Ian, he took a copy of your passport."

"Yes, that was me." He nodded. "My surname is Saint. I was born sixty-six years ago in Germany in a British Army base hospital near Berlin. I've lived here in the UK and abroad, I've done all the things I have told you. Those were my friends." A tear rolled down his cheek

Christos spoke for the first time, his tone curt. "Passports can be falsified. I should know." Johnny held up his hands in mock surrender.

"Look, you need to decide for yourselves who you believe me to be. I cannot tell you. It must come from you. To help you decide, take this." Johnny got up, went to a drawer in the kitchen, and took out two small test tubes with rubber bungs. The kind you get in a children's chemistry set. He sat back down and proceeded to spit into one of the tubes. He sealed it up. In the other, he placed several strands of hair that he plucked from his head, wincing as he did so. He handed them to Sam. "Get the DNA tested. Apparently, you can match up the chronological age with the biological age, within reason. You will be able to tell if the DNA is sixty or so years old or two thousand. That will help you decide."

"Johnny, you are my friend, just tell me. Are you him?" Sam almost pleaded.

"If I said yes, and was lying, then what? If I said no and was lying, then what? If I told you, I was he and it was true, then what? No, you must have the evidence and make up your own mind. Now, let's get down to planning how to stop Satan's warriors from killing me eh?" He grinned.

THIRTY-SEVEN

The remainder of the weekend passed without incident, Sam decided to refrain from telling Sally about Mel and Robert until after Mel had left on Sunday afternoon. They sat around the kitchen table and Sally poured herself another large glass of wine.

"I still can't believe this," she said, sipping her New Zealand Sauvignon Blanc. She picked up some of the photographs that Christos had printed from his phone and the transcript of the conversations he had recorded, flicking through them repeatedly, just to make sure she had all the facts right.

"It all fits; Digamma is a front for the activities of The Six, worldwide. I suspect there are branches of The Six on each continent. We need Robert Frost's laptop or PC to confirm connections, but we can identify possible 'Six' members from the global websites." Christos was leading the discussion; his experience in intelligence made him the natural choice. "I have spoken to my contacts in MI5 and handed over the data we have. They were both impressed and troubled that I had managed to discover this when their efforts had heralded no results.

Christos picked up the two small test tubes and held them up. "As for these, I will take them personally to the Greek Embassy tomorrow where they can have them tested more rapidly than through conventional methods. We will discover who our friend Johnny Saint really is."

With suspiciously perfect timing Sam's phone buzzed. He picked up from the table nonchalantly and glanced at the screen. His eyes widened and a look of panic spread over his face as if he had seen a ghost. He turned the screen around to reveal the name of the person calling. Robert Frost.

"Answer it!" Christos whispered as if Frost could hear him.

Sam pressed the green button and the speaker button so everyone could hear, and spoke as confidently as he could. "Robert, good to hear from you. How are you doing? It must be so difficult for you."

"Sam, my old friend, it is good to hear your voice. To be honest I am struggling. Suzanne's death has hit me hard. I need someone I can talk to. I need a break, time away from the desk. I know this is an imposition, that we haven't been in contact for years but can I come and stay?"

In the room, there was a rapid series of nods. Sally shook her head, concern written large on her face. Christos nodded furiously encouraging Sam to say yes. Maria sided with Sally; a slight shake of her head was all that was needed. After what seemed like an age, Sam responded.

"Sorry for the delay, Robert, I just had to check my calendar." He paused and then took a deep breath. "Yes, that would be lovely. I am free for a couple of days from Tuesday." The conversation continued for a minute more, with the address and directions being given, and then a little more small talk before the call ended. Sally had a face like thunder.

"What the hell did you do that for? He's a bloody terrorist!"

Christos responded before Sam could reply. "It is better he is here and we know what he wants than be taken by surprise. Besides it means I can search his house whilst he is here." He grinned. Sally puffed out her cheeks. "I don't like it." She stood up and left the kitchen.

"Right," said Christos, "we have about 24 hours to plan." Sam looked at him nervously and thought; *have I just let the Devil into my home?*

The Chairman closed the call on his mobile and sat back in the high-backed oak carver chair in the small conference room attached to his office in Whitehall. It was quiet on a Sunday afternoon and the five other members of the European branch of Digamma resumed their meeting.

"Apologies for the length of the call, but as you can see, I am playing a part. Sometimes you need to overact it. I will be away for a few days discovering what this meddling estate agent really knows. The secretary has done a good job and has worked her way into this family. They believe her to be a victim of The Six rather than a key component. The remainder of those present all turned to face Melanie Chambers, who nodded and smiled sweetly. There was a lascivious look from Lydia Raymond, the tall black, medal-winning athlete. She winked at Melanie and licked her top lip erotically. Melanie received the message gratefully. Thomas Dexter the local Police Commissioner went one step further. "I congratulate you Melanie; perhaps we can meet up later when I can show you my appreciation properly?

"I would love that, Tom." Melanie's voice oozed sexuality. "You have my number." She smiled again, coyly."

"Please can we refrain from letting our animal urges dictate our meetings?" The voice was sharp and stern. It came from Celia Hartington, an actor in her early seventies, for whom the pleasures of sex had largely passed her by. "I congratulate you Melanie, but I have no desire to see inside your underwear! I know that we are not used to seeing each other's faces and knowing identities but we need some sense of decorum." She was old school and preferred to keep her vices private. She drank heavily, used recreational drugs and spent much of her wealth on the horses.

"Celia, thank you for your candour. You are right of course. The younger ones tend to think with their sex organs rather than their brains! There will be time to spend indulging yourselves as you wish. But now is not the time or place to organise it." The Chairman spoke calmly, yet Lydia's advances to Melanie intrigued him. He would like to see that play out. He had to concentrate hard to prevent images from flooding his mind.

The meeting continued all afternoon with Duncan Masterson, the Administrator and the CEO of a large electronic technology firm, sharing his plan to undermine confidence in the Muslim community, with a series of terror attacks on Christian Churches by Islamist extremists. He also shared how his funding of far-right Christian political groups was allowing them to spread fear among moderate Christians regarding 'the influence of the Muslim infidels' and the 'cancer of the gay rights agenda.' Both of these brought ripples of applause from the others gathered in the small conference room. Similar meetings were taking place around the globe as Digamma planned the next round of 'charitable events.'

THIRTY-EIGHT

Johnny Saint stood leaning on his garden fork; he watched from the kitchen garden of Downs Wood Farm. It was more the size of seven or eight allotments arranged with a variety of beds for growing fruit and vegetables, with an orchard of apple trees alongside it. There was a large polytunnel and several smaller ones that housed tomatoes, peppers cucumbers and the like, all in varying stages of development. Sam wanted year-round crops to supply the small farm shop. Outside in the beds, a small army of volunteers was harvesting the crops ready for sale. The wind blowing up the valley tempered the autumn sunshine. Johnny shivered as he watched the JCB digging a deep foundation for the toilet and shower block across the field in what was soon to be the Downs Wood Farm Glamping site. The site was littered with recently dug trenches. Soil and water pipes, electric cables and even TV cables were about to be laid. It reminded him of a time long ago when the landscape was ripped up by man's inhumanity to man.

Sam arrived and disturbed Johnny's peaceful reflection of an age past.

"Hey, Johnny, where was your mind just then? I've been calling you from across the garden." Sam smiled warmly.

"Sorry Sam, just taking a moment." He stood up straight and turned to greet his friend.

"It's fine. A man as old as you needs to take regular rests." Sam patted him on the shoulder in jest. "Now, how far should we extend the kitchen garden? I would like to have soft fruit beds and even a kids' play area."

"How about a café attached to the shop? Homemade cakes and bacon sandwiches." Johnny was teasing him.

"Hey, that's not bad, I like it." Sam was genuine. He began to explore the area needed and took photos with his camera. They wandered the area discussing potential ideas for extension.

"Sally will love it; she and Kelly could run it. It would attract more people to the glamping site if there were breakfasts and dinners on tap."

"Sam, slow down." Johnny grabbed his arm and stood facing him. "We have to deal with your friend Robert and The Six before you plan a future. You're mixed up in something very dangerous and you must find a way of dealing with it, to protect Sally, yourself and your friends. If what you say is true, they will not stop until they have eradicated religious beliefs or found this apostle John."

Sam looked him in the eye and gave a wry smile. Johnny smiled too.

"You're not going to tell me are you?" Johnny shook his head. "You're right, of course. Robert Frost is arriving tonight. I suspect he wants to find out what I know, whether I am a threat or if I know anything about you!" He playfully poked Johnny in the chest. It was Johnny's turn to give the wry smile. "Meanwhile, Christos will find the evidence to convince MI5 to get involved, and then we will be free of it all."

At the same time as Robert Frost slung his overnight bag in the boot of his Jaguar F-Pace and pulled out of his driveway in north London, just as the sun was going down, Christos Megalos broke into the local electricity substation. He planted a small radio-controlled device that would generate a low-energy microwave pulse that would disrupt the electrical supply and short-circuit it cutting the power to the local area. By the time Frost was on the M23 heading toward Brighton, Christos had cut the electricity, rendering all Frost's alarms and cameras useless, broken into his home undetected and inserted a small chip into Frost's laptop enabling him to see everything he did on it and send it directly to Sam's server.

THIRTY-NINE

Frost pulled up in the yard of Downs Wood Farm. It was dark and his headlights swept the yard, reflecting in the windows of the farm shop. He was wary of his old friend, unsure if he was a threat to The Six or not. He had no desire to kill him or his beautiful wife, but he would if Sam got in the way. He sat in the car for a moment and composed himself, drawing down the mask of respectability until he was ready to play the part of Robert Frost, grieving widower and Prime Minister's aide. The front door of the farmhouse opened and Sam stood silhouetted in the frame. Frost stepped out of the car, retrieved his bag and walked up to greet his old friend.

"Sam, I am so glad you were able to accommodate an old fool like me." Frost smiled genially as he spoke.

"Enough of the old, we're the same age!" He slapped his friend on the shoulder. "Welcome to Downs Wood Farm. Come in and say hello to Sally. There are a few others that I'd like you to meet as well."

Sam led him into the lounge and Sally greeted him with a smile. "Robert, so good to see you. How are you bearing up?" She leaned in and they kissed cheek to cheek.

"I'm surviving," he lied. "To be honest it is hard, especially as the killer is still on the loose." Sally nodded sympathetically.

"Robert, let me introduce you to Ian and Kelly; they help me run the estate. And this is Maria, a friend from Greece; we met in the summer. Her husband Christos should be back soon. He had to go to London, to meet a client. He is a property investor and restaurateur." Robert shook hands and nodded politely as the introductions were made.

"Bobby," Sam turned to his boyhood pal, "does anyone call you Bobby anymore?"

"No, it is generally Robert. But go ahead. It reminds me of a time when life was less complicated."

"Bobby, make yourself at home," Sam gestured to a chair and Frost sat down.

"Can I get you a drink? It's late, so perhaps a scotch to round the night off? I have this marvellous 13-year-old single malt called Mortlach. Anyone else need a top-up?" There were nods, and Sally went around replenishing glasses whilst Sam poured out a generous measure of Mortlach for Robert.

"Cheers! To old friends, to loved ones lost and new beginnings." Sam raised his glass as did all in the room. Robert Frost took it all in, playing his part supremely well.

The sound of wheels on gravel and the searching beams of headlights alerted them to the arrival of Christos. By the time introductions were made and more whisky had been drunk, it was past one in the morning when Robert Frost found himself alone in one of the guest bedrooms. He brushed his teeth and flicked off the light in the en-suite. Slipping into bed, he reached for his phone and opened up his texting app. He began texting a message.

> R u sure they know about John?
> Seem stupid. Will try to flush them out tomorrow?
> Inform others of progress as and when.

Then as an afterthought, he added;

> Could do with u right now x

He thought of The Secretary, Melanie, and he felt the stirrings of arousal. His animal instincts were hard to control. He hit send on his phone and began to wonder if Sally or Maria could satisfy his needs. It only made matters worse as his mind played out a range of warped scenarios.

His phone pinged and he opened the message. There was a simple message.

Very sure.

Seconds later the phone pinged again and this time there was a photo of Melanie Chambers in a pose that was well-suited to any porno site. It was followed by a simple message.

Ready when U R

Robert Frost was unaware that, as well as inserting a chip into his laptop, Christos had gathered all his passwords from his password manager and was currently monitoring his text conversation from Sam's office. He grinned from ear to ear as the picture of Melanie Chambers appeared on screen.

FORTY

Sam, Ian and Robert had spent the morning touring the farm and Sam gushed as he explained his development plans. The day was overcast and a storm was approaching. The clouds swirled and danced as the wind pushed them across the sky. Sam was busy pointing out the foundations for the new toilet block and Robert feigned interest, asking questions and looking earnestly wherever Sam pointed out things. However, there came a point when he could take no more of Sam's enthusiastic chatter about the banality of his life. Frost needed to know his involvement in the hunt for the apostle John. At that moment, Johnny Saint rode past on a quad bike pulling a trailer full of vegetables bound for the barn to be cleaned, ready for the shop. In an attempt to pull the conversation away from glamping and shower blocks, Robert Frost almost shouted.

"Who's that?" He pointed at the man on the quad bike. Sam hesitated, wondering how to respond. He had asked Johnny to keep out of sight; he did not even want Frost suspecting that he may be harbouring anyone.

"Aah! That's someone Ian hired as a temporary hand. He's renting the flat above the shop."

Ian chipped in, to give credence to the statement. "Yes, he's quite new, here for a few weeks to help out over harvest. We need someone more permanent." Frost seemed satisfied and they moved on. As they approached the farmhouse, Frost began to question Sam.

"Tell me Sam, what about your writing? I hear you are publishing a second book. About one of Jesus's disciples, is that right?" He tried to make it sound casual, but Sam picked up the note of stress in his voice.

"I wasn't aware you knew about my writing." Sam stopped and

faced his friend. "It is more of a hobby than a career."

"I'm in the Civil Service, it pays to know things. Sometimes it gives a person an edge." He smiled but it did not reach his eyes. Sam nodded understanding.

"I wrote a book about English myths and legends. You know the kind of stuff. Robin Hood, Glastonbury, the chalice, King Arthur," he gestured with his hands. "For some reason, it did well and the publisher asked me to write about the Apostle John. I like Biblical history, I find it fascinating, and so I agreed. It will never be a best seller."

"Unless, of course, they find him alive!" Frost held his ground and stared at Sam. This was the crunch point. Sam knew it was coming. He was waiting for Frost to make his play. He wasn't going to give him anything.

"Alive? Who?" Sam played dumb very well. Sally always thought he was a natural. He tried hard to remain calm and casual.

"John, the myth of chapter 21. Jesus said John wouldn't die until he returned."

Sam snorted and feigned surprise.

"What? That's nonsense, just a legend. There is no reason to take it seriously. No proper theological scholar would even countenance the idea that Jesus actually kept John alive." He tried to brush it off as quickly as possible but Frost didn't bite.

"No evidence! You haven't done your research Sam, there is plenty out there."

"I didn't realise you were so interested. As I recall as a kid you hated all that religious stuff." Sam tried to put him off balance.

"That was because of what happened to me, the Church let me down. If, however, something is true, then let it be verified so all can share in the truth."

"Do you believe John the Apostle is alive?" Sam tried to make his words sound mocking, "You really think a two-thousand-year-old man is wandering about the planet somewhere?"

By now, they found themselves in the kitchen, Sam making coffee.

"That's not what I said. I want to know if you think he is alive. That is what your book is about, isn't it?" Sam handed him a coffee and placed a plate of biscuits on the table. He picked one up and dunked it in his coffee then popped the whole thing in his mouth. It gave him time to think.

"No, my book is about the life and work of the apostle John. The legend of Ch. 21 is just a footnote at the end. Or will be when it is written." He smiled at Frost wanting to imply that Frost's theories about John were misplaced.

"You have travelled all over Europe in John's footsteps; you must have found some evidence of the legend." As soon as he spoke, Frost realised he had slipped up. How was he supposed to know Sam's movements? It didn't go unnoticed. Sam noticed it but filed it away for later. He made no acknowledgement of it.

"True, Sally and I spent the summer in Europe, but it was mainly a holiday with a little research. Yes, some people believe the legend, but there is no concrete evidence of it being true." Sam sat back and sipped his coffee. He watched as Frost picked up a digestive and dunked it. He quickly bit off the soggy part and swallowed it fast. Maria entered the kitchen, holding Thomas on her hip. She greeted them both and went to the fridge to find some lunch for her son. Sam noticed how Frost's eyes followed Maria around. His eyes were dark and without warmth but there was a lustful look on his face, just for a moment. Sam watched as he licked his lips. He could not decide whether it was crumbs or lust that made him do it. A slight shudder ran down Sam's back as if he were in the presence of evil.

"Bobby, tell me, your role as the PM's aide must give you insight into all sorts of issues going on in the UK, the world in fact." Frost was taken aback by the sudden change of topic. He pulled his gaze away from Maria and refocused on Sam.

"Well, yes, I suppose so. Most of it is classified of course." Sam steered the conversation away from John to see if he would steer it back. They sat for thirty minutes discussing Frost's role as aide to the PM of the UK. They metaphorically danced around each other. Neither one wanted to slip up and give away any information. Each one trying to convince the other of their innocence and ignorance of John, The Six and terrorist attacks on the UK mainland.

"Is it true, Bobby, that there is a secret terror organisation behind these anti-religious attacks? National News seemed to think so in a recent report I saw on the TV." Sam took the plunge wanting to gauge his reaction. There was a flicker in his eye before he responded, that told Sam he was about to lie.

"No such thing. The PM has investigated this using all of the UK's intelligence networks and we can find no evidence of any organisation. That is all I can say. I wouldn't trust anyone you see on the telly." Frost's voice carried authority; you wanted to believe him. Sam smiled inwardly and thought. *Good advice! Your girlfriend, Melanie Chambers for a start.*

"That's strange," Sam retorted, "the serious news outlets are generally spot on when it comes to this kind of intelligence." Sam wanted to push him into an error without giving away his own position of knowledge.

"I wouldn't waste too much time on all this Sam; there is no mysterious organisation at work here. Focus on setting up your campsite and get back to your business. Finish your writing, but remember, as you say, John is a myth." It was spoken genially but It sounded like a warning.

Just then, Sally arrived from her stint in the shop. She carried fresh bread and eggs and was ready to cook.

"Lunch anyone?" she smiled, acting the role of a happy host, but underneath there was a deep mistrust of Robert Frost.

FORTY-ONE

Three days later, Robert Frost led a conference of all thirty-six key trustees of the worldwide charity called Digamma. They sat in a large conference room kitted out with a TV monitor linked to a laptop. The desks had headed notepaper and pencils for each delegate and a table of refreshments filled with an array of pastries, tea and coffee was laid out at the back of the room. Digamma banners promoting the official charity adorned the walls. They were one of many conferences and trade shows attending an international event in the 'Moscone Center', San Francisco. It was the perfect cover. The centre was heaving with visitors of all sorts, trade delegations, charity representatives, religious groups, sci-fi enthusiasts and much more. No one would notice thirty-six, hooded figures milling around among the host of guests. Each of the trustees had arrived separately, and stayed at different hotels, to protect their identities. As far as Frost knew, his European 'Six' were the only ones who had identified themselves to each other. The charade of the hoods was an ancient tradition that Frost believed to be unnecessary, almost religious. The fact that his face and that of the five other UK trustees of Digamma appeared on their official website made a mockery of the secrecy of the hoods. Yet the others insisted, so he played along.

He looked at the thirty-five other hooded figures sitting around the conference table. Small labels in front of them denoted their role and region. His eyes lingered on the Chairman of the Middle East delegation. Once again his animal instincts kicked in and he wondered what she might look like beneath the hood, and even naked.

"Ladies and Gentleman, thank you for giving up your time to attend the first of what I hope to be an annual gathering until our mutual quest is complete. The charity *Digamma* provides us with an excellent cover and we must ensure that remains intact and is reputable and law-abiding. Please continue to arrange, support and finance a wide range of events that promote scientific and rational understanding of the planet. We must deflect any suspicion away from us at all times. In the meantime, whilst we are together we must plan for the downfall of religious beliefs of all kinds through terror, murder and political manipulation." The Chairman paused, ensuring engagement from all trustees in the room.

"I believe it is time we dispensed with secrecy. I know it is an ancient tradition of the Atomists. But how can we enjoy each other's company and share in each other's pleasures if we remain unknown to each other? I propose we lower our hoods. The European sector has already done so. We are known to each other." With that, the European 'Six' members pulled back their hoods to reveal their faces.

"Now, hang on a minute," the North American, New York accent sounded anxious.

"I gotta reputation to keep. I ain't lettin' anyone in on my identity."

"Mr Schaeffer, you are the CEO of a giant oil company, and you live in a penthouse in New York's 5th Avenue." The voice was female and had a definite Middle Eastern tone. The room turned as one to the Chairman of the Middle Eastern sector. Delicate tanned hands lifted her hood from her head and revealed the face of Middle Eastern Origin. She was classically beautiful with jet-black shoulder-length hair, and olive-toned skin. Her make-up highlighted her high cheekbones and the strong eyeliner gave depth and beauty to her eyes.

"What the fu...." Schaeffer never finished his sentence. He was dumbstruck by her beauty.

"How did you know who I was?" He tried to regain his composure.

"You are a very public figure, Mr Schaeffer. Your voice is

recognisable. I agree with the European contingent. We must dispense with ancient traditions. After all, we are not a religion." Several people laughed. Even Schaeffer. Slowly the figures around the table lowered their hoods as the absurdity of their tradition became real. Robert Frost, the Chairman of the European Sector smiled. It was all coming together. His hopes about the Chairman of the Middle Eastern sector were realised. She was indeed someone with whom he would like to be intimate. More importantly, he had succeeded in getting everyone to reveal his or her face. Unbeknown to them all, the TV monitor situated behind his head was in fact a prototype recorder and monitor being trialled at the very exhibition they were attending. A little friendly coercion had persuaded the sales rep of the company to let him trial it in "a charity meeting so that there is a visual record of the meeting for all." The salesperson was more than happy to oblige given that Frost bought one and asked for it to be shipped to the UK. *Money well spent* he thought, as the images of all their faces were now his to keep. Leverage in case some people became less than enthusiastic about what he was about to ask.

Frost surveyed the room. He recognised many of the faces, celebrities, politicians, and businesspersons from all across the globe. Here were the next generation of world leaders, those who would take control of key institutions and industries once the collapse of the current world system was complete. There would be a vacuum when faith in God and religion were discredited. Digamma needed to be ready to step in and offer people a new, self-centred and elitist way of life that gave power, wealth and pleasure to the strongest and most able. The fulfilment of the basest human desires.

"My fellow atomists, our search for the Apostle John continues. I believe him to be alive and his whereabouts to be known by this man and his wife. He pressed a button on his laptop and Sam and Sally's faces appeared on the monitor behind his head. I will concentrate on this aspect of our mission with my European colleagues. Each of the other sectors must increase your activity tenfold to create as much chaos, unrest and mistrust as possible. I want the New Year to be a time of radical development for our cause. Increase attacks on religious buildings, lobby for restrictions of faith activities, and organise assassinations of key religious figures. I suggest we target the Pope, the Dalai Llama, the Archbishop of Canterbury, the leader of the Sephardi Jews and finally the King of Saudi Arabia. In terms of historic sites, we need to destroy the Dome of the Rock and make it look like Zionists were responsible. An attack on the Kaaba would be a challenge but well worth it. I expect we could blame American Evangelicals for that one!" There were ripples of laughter from the assembled.

The meeting continued for a further two hours, with discussions on tactics, plans and specific targets. By the time the meeting ended, the future of the world's faiths hung in the balance. The Six were set to destroy them all.

The meeting formally closed and the members of Digamma began to mingle. Frost noticed Melanie flirting with an American musician famous for his rock ballads. He smiled. *Good luck to her.* He made his way swiftly towards the stunning Chairperson of the Middle Eastern Sector. She stood alone. He held out his hand in greeting.

"I don't think we have been formally introduced. I am Robert Frost, Personal Aide to the British Prime Minister" She smiled and shook his hand.

"I am Nadia Safar; I am a businesswoman from Jordan. I run an export business focussing on clothing, mainly knitted or handmade." Deep down in the darkest part of his heart, Frost knew he would not be satisfied until he had conquered this extraordinary woman.

"May we have dinner together? Now that the foolishness of secrecy is over."

"I am not sure it is completely over." She pointed to the door. "It seems our American friends still want to play." Schaeffer and the entire North American sector had covered themselves before leaving. Other sectors were doing the same as if their resolve from earlier had dissipated.

"Eight o'clock in my suite at the Hilton. We will dine in private and I will gladly show off my stock." She winked as she turned from Frost, flicked up her hood and left the room. Frost was still grinning like the cat who got the cream when he realised he was alone in the room. Quickly he shut down his laptop, disconnected it from the monitor and left the room. He failed to cover his head in his elation at the thought of sex with Nadia.

On a balcony overlooking the entrance to the conference room, a woman with a long-lensed camera snapped his image.

"That's the last one. About half had hoods, but the others we should be able to identify. Sending over images now." She spoke quietly into a tiny microphone clipped to her lapel.

"Copy that." A crackly voice responded in her ear.

"Copy that? Who are you supposed to be, the FBI?" Sally put down the camera and spoke casually into her lapel.

"Sorry darling got carried away. I expect Edna can identify all these images; we should have enough for Christos to pass on to MI5 and give them something to follow up on."

"What if they don't bite? What will we do then?"

"Let's cross that bridge when we come to it, eh? In the meantime, I will meet you back at the hotel in an hour. I need to see where Frost is staying. I am on his trail. Tucker out!"

Sally laughed, "Numpty." She saw the hooded figure of Frost walking through the main exhibition area, and then her eyes caught sight of Sam, trying to be discreet as he followed Frost towards the main doors.

"My contacts in MI5, Greek intelligence, and even in Interpol all say that this is not enough. Photos of delegates leaving a legitimate charity trustee meeting. There is no evidence of wrongdoing. No one in that meeting has done anything to break the law. Not all of the delegates have yet been identified. Of those we know, they are upstanding members of the worldwide community. Initial investigations show no evidence of criminal activity."

"As far as we know!" Sam was becoming agitated. Sam was on a Zoom call with Christos, who was back in Patmos with Maria and Thomas. "There must be more that we can do. Can we flush them out; make them reveal their identity somehow?" Sam, Sally, Ian, Kelly and Johnny sat around the kitchen table each with their own tablet or phone, connected to the meeting.

"You could always use me as bait," Johnny spoke quietly and slowly. "If they are so intent on finding the apostle John, then let's give them something to get excited about."

"No chance!" Sam was adamant. Sally and the others agreed. "We're not putting you in danger Johnny, that's madness."

Christos spoke. "It may be our only way. You want to flush them out. Then give them Johnny, by accident of course. Let Melanie know you think that your new employee is the same person as Johnny Heiliger, the missing link from Berlin. Send her a photo. Do it in all innocence. Remember, they don't know that you understand who they are. She believes that you think she is on your side."

"What will that achieve?" Ian spoke up.

"If they take the bait, then they will come for him. Either in person or send some thugs." Christos laid the plan out in full.

"That is too dangerous. It will put Johnny and potentially all of us at risk." Sally's voice revealed the fear in her voice. "This is getting deadly."

"I will be here, covertly. I will protect him, and you. All we need to do is get them to act. Then MI5 and all the others will respond."

The arguments went back and forth for several minutes until Johnny interjected.

"Listen, this was my idea initially. It should be my call. If I leave the farm, then it will keep you safe."

"No way, we all agreed to help each other. We can't abandon Johnny now." It was the first time Kelly had really spoken, but she had brought clarity to the confused discussion. "Friendship goes beyond safety. We stick by each other. How about we let Melanie know about Johnny a couple of days before Bonfire Night? We've invited the whole village here for a party. It will be buzzing. A perfect cover for kidnap, but easier for us to control the exits and block them when necessary." The room went quiet, even Christos in Patmos was still. Everyone stared at her. "What? I read a lot of thrillers. You just pick things up." It broke the tension.

Johnny sat back in the chair closed his eyes and whispered a silent prayer. *Oh Lord, I hope I have done the right thing here. Protect us all from harm. End this evil.*

"Johnny, are you okay with all this? We don't have to do this. We can find another way." Sam looked at his old friend and mentor, sitting eyes closed.

He opened them and smiled. "I'm all in. We need to end this once and for all." The meeting closed and then the task of planning began. By the time they all retired to bed, it was past midnight.

FORTY-TWO

At nine am on Wednesday 3rd November, Sam sent Robert Frost an email with a last-minute invitation to the Downs Wood Farm village bonfire. A small flier was attached to the email outlining that the event was open to all those who lived in Alfriston and their friends. There would be food stalls with local produce, a makeshift bar, a hog roast and of course, a bonfire and firework display, all on the grounds of Downs Wood Farm.

Later that evening, Sally sent what appeared to be a casual text message to Melanie Chambers with a photo of Johnny Saint.

Hi Mel

LOL! Sam thinks he's found the apostle John. His old mate Johnny Saint. Now works on the farm. Says he looks a bit like that bloke from the German Church who went missing.

I don't think so, do you?

PS We're having a village bonfire party on Friday evening. Fancy coming down? We can introduce you to the apostle. Ha! Ha! xx

She put a couple of laughing emojis after the message and then sent a picture of Johnny Saint sitting on his four-by-four buggy.

That evening there was an emergency Zoom meeting of the European 'Six'. Frost sat in his study on his laptop. Five other faces appeared on the screen.

"It seems our friends in Sussex have found the missing apostle, even if it was by accident." Frost shared the photo of Johnny Saint and then a photo of Johan Heiliger next to it.

"Initial research suggests he appeared in Sussex days after we attempted to flush him out in Germany. There are clear similarities; he even uses a very poor pseudonym, 'Johnny

Saint'." There were ripples of laughter from the five familiar faces on Frost's laptop screen.

"I have already initiated a plan that will enable us to capture Johnny Saint whilst his friends are otherwise engaged in a bonfire party at their farm. It will be the perfect cover. I will send operatives to kidnap him and detain him until we can verify his identity. We, of course, will maintain our distance. Although I like a good bonfire." Again, there were ripples of laughter.

"Mr. Chairman, how can you be certain that Sam Tucker is not setting us up? You said yourself he appeared to have an unhealthy interest in John and even suggested that an organisation such as ours could exist. Should we risk such exposure? Surely it is better to wait, gather more intelligence and create a more subtle way of making Johnny Saint disappear." Thomas Dexter, the Treasurer and senior ranking police officer, spoke cautiously. He understood the Chairman's passion but also his impatience.

"Thomas, my friend, please do not think I am being impatient, or rash. I understand your police training and see it appearing here, but note this. If you challenge me again in such a public way, I will ensure that the public will know of your secrets. Your passion for children. I assume you still have all those photographs hidden on your hard drive?" Thomas Dexter went pale.

"How? How did you…" His voice cracked.

"Thomas," he smiled. "I know everyone's secrets. I would be foolish if I didn't hold all the cards. I know secrets about you all." He could see the other four beginning to feel uncomfortable and knew his message had hit home.

"Now, where were we?"

In Sam's study, on Downs Wood Farm a little red light flashed indicating the server was receiving a new data upload.

FORTY-THREE

In typical fashion, the weather leading up to November 5th had been wet. Very wet. Preparations for the bonfire event had been slow. Throughout the day vans arrived, and stalls, food outlets and the hog roast were set up. Makeshift walkways were installed to prevent the sodden fields from excess damage. As the day progressed, the weather improved and all was set for what was to be an exciting night of food, drink and fireworks. A team of volunteers helped all day and by the time 5 pm arrived and the villagers began to arrive the farm looked like a fairground. The smell of roast pork filled the air, and several braziers lit the way to the main field, each one staffed by a person in a thick overcoat and hat to keep the November chill out. Lights from the stalls and food outlets created a carnival atmosphere and music pumped out of speakers located at strategic points around the farm. Children chattered and ran about with balloons; parents carried toddlers who wiggled their arms and legs in delight. Couples walked hand in hand around the range of stalls, stopping to browse the local fare. Young men headed for the bar where local ales were on sale at reduced prices, thanks to Sam's generosity. The bonfire was like a beacon, a hundred metres down the field, roped off and guarded by some local farmers. It lit up the sky, creating an orange luminescence with the occasional explosion of sparks lighting up the night sky.

Sam, Sally, Ian and Kelly all had radios and kept in contact with each other. Ian sat in the tractor by the main gate ready to block the gate if anyone tried to make a getaway with Johnny in a van or car. Kelly sat at the highest window in the farmhouse. In the loft space. A skylight overlooked the courtyard. She had a set of night vision goggles acquired by Christos. She could see the shop, the entrance to Johnny's apartment, the fields beyond with the stalls and of course, the yard where any cars might arrive. Sam wandered the event acting as a genial host. Sally was in the shop, supervising the staff and keeping an eye on the apartment.

Johnny sat in his apartment with Christos. The plan was to contain any attempt to kidnap him within the flat and not disrupt the event.

By six o'clock the event was in full swing. Well over three hundred people were milling around enjoying a surprisingly dry evening. It was sticky underfoot on the field and wellies were the best footwear. Most of the locals had walked or parked in the lanes around the farm.

Static crackled on Sam's radio followed by the sound of Ian's voice. "Black van, Volkswagen Caddie just pulled up in the yard, taken the space we intended." Ian pressed a button on a remote, and from the kitchen window, a high-powered night camera whirred into life.

Two men got out and one went around the back and opened the rear door. Another man scrambled out. They shut the doors of the van.

"Three men, dressed in dark clothing, short bomber jackets, zipped up. Shit! They have guns. All three have just produced automatic pistols, checked them and tucked them back into waistbands at the rear of their jackets," Ian's voice sounded panicky.

Christos' voice came over the airwaves. "Let them move off and then position the tractor. Keep me informed of movements."

"I have them in sight!" said Kelly. "These goggles are awesome!"

"Where are they headed?" Sam asked with an urgency in his voice.

"They're putting on ski masks!" Kelly seemed to be shouting from her vantage point in the loft room. "They're going straight for the apartment."

Sam set off at a pace back towards the main courtyard of the farm. The three men entered the farm shop. There were screams and shouting as the men ordered Sally, the staff and 3 customers down on the floor. One of them stayed in the shop, his angry eyes darting between his hostages and he continually changed his aim ensuring all his charges remained as still as the dead. The other two scurried beyond the counter to the stairs leading to the apartment and estate office.

"What's going on? What are you doing? Take the money!" Sally, although genuinely scared, played the part well. She lay on the floor wondering if her phone that she had placed on the shelf behind the counter was still upright and recording. It was. She thought of Sam, praying that he wouldn't burst in. The walkie-talkie crackled with static and a muffled voice sounded.

"What's that?" The masked gunman shouted and pointed his automatic directly at Sally. "Who is it?" He picked up the radio from the counter and then knelt beside Sally. "Sit up, carefully. Any sudden movements and I will kill you." His breath was stale and he smelt unwashed. Sally carefully manoeuvred into a sitting position and waited for instruction. The radio crackled again. This time the voice had clarity.

"This is Tucker 1, checking in. All good on the dance floor. All units check in please."

"What's that about, what's going on?" The gunman pushed the pistol close to Sally's cheek.

"Why have you got radios? What is the code?" For the first time, Sally noticed the man's accent; it was Eastern European.

"Look around you, there is a big social event going on. There are hundreds of people here. It is just my husband playing with his toys, checking the staff are on duty." The gunman hesitated and looked around at the scared faces. Something clicked in his mind. He motioned to Sally, "Get up, lock the shop door." Make sure no one comes in. You try and run, I will kill someone, maybe you. Radio your husband and tell him all is ok. No tricks!" He handed Sally the Radio. She raised herself up off the floor and put the radio close to her mouth.

"Tucker 1 this is Tucker 2, all well in the shop. Over." Even in this dire strait, she felt stupid calling herself Tucker 2. It was Sam's way of trying to make light of the situation. *Muppet.* She slowly moved toward the door and dropped the latch. She turned the sign from 'open' to 'closed'. Kelly watched through the night vision goggles from her vantage point in the loft. She switched radio channels and called Sam.

"Sam, Sally has just closed the shop; I think it's going down now."

FORTY-FOUR

Inside the apartment, Johnny and Christos were listening in. Johnny sat on the sofa; the TV was on with the sound low. Christos waited in the toilet just inside the front door of the apartment the door ajar and the light off. With any luck, the intruders would run straight to where Johnny was sitting, ignoring any dark rooms.

Outside the apartment, the two other masked gunmen arrived. They listened for sounds and could just about hear the sound of a television. One of them tried the handle of the apartment door, which Christos had conveniently left on the latch. He wanted to make it easy for them. Slowly and very quietly, like ghosts, the two gunmen entered the apartment. They passed the toilet where Christos hid and moved silently towards the door to the main living room. Stepping out of the toilet, Christos followed equally silently. His military and intelligence training served him well. When he reached the living room door, he surveyed the scene. The two gunmen had their backs to him. Both had raised their guns. Johnny stood facing them, his hands in the air. He desperately tried not to look beyond the men to where Christos stood so as not to give away his position.

"What do you want?" His voice was calm. He wanted to keep their attention as long as he could. "I don't have money, but take the TV." He tried to sound a little scared but it was not in his nature to feel fear, only trust in the God who had rescued him so many times.

One of them spoke; "We have come for you, Apostle John." His voice was also Eastern European. He was tall and thin and his black jacket hung loosely on him, as if he needed a good meal. John shook his head in disbelief.

"I think you have made a mistake my friends." He held out his hands in an open gesture.

"Hands back up!" the other shouted. John obeyed and out of the corner of his eye watched Christos manoeuvre himself behind one of the men. Whilst pointing a pistol at the gunman's head he fired a Taser into the back of the other. With a sudden writhing movement and shriek, the gunman dropped his weapon and fell to the floor quivering. The second gunman turned to find Christos immediately behind him. With a swift blow, Christos struck him across the face, the butt of his pistol catching his nose. Blood exploded from it and the man screamed as he fell clutching his nose. Johnny moved swiftly to pick up the guns whilst Christos tied the men up with police issue zip-tie restraints. He stuffed tissue up the bleeding nostrils of the injured gunman having removed his mask. He yelped as it came over his shattered nose. Christos told him to breathe through his mouth. The Tasered gunman was just coming around. He trembled as Christos removed his mask. He was pale; all fight had gone from him. The effect of the 50,000 volts in his body.

Christos stepped over to the coffee table and picked up the walkie-talkie; "Tucker 1, this is Tucker 3, two assailants incapacitated and secured. I will call in the cavalry to collect them and the third waiting downstairs. I am sure he will surrender without a fight." Christos smiled, knowing that the third gunman would be listening in. He spoke again. "I repeat this is Tucker 3, two assailants secured and waiting upstairs for collection. I suspect the third is about to make a run for it." Outside, three of the men guarding the braziers left their posts, and discarded their heavy overcoats, scarves and hats, revealing dark, police-like jackets with an NPSA logo on the front and NPSA in big letters on the back, similar to those worn by the FBI or any other US government agency. Christos had pulled in some favours from his contacts in MI5. Three members of the National Protective Security Authority had been dispatched to support Christos' covert operation. He had convinced an old friend there was a credible risk. His assessment had now been confirmed. They pulled out automatic weapons and headed off towards the shop.

FORTY-FIVE

As Christos spoke to the NPSA officers over the radio, the third gunman was panicking. He had heard the message, and as his friends had not returned, he correctly surmised that the message had been accurate. He looked around, fear emanating from him. He grabbed Sally and pushed her towards the door. "Unlock it!" he barked, pointing the pistol in her face. Sally scurried over to the door and unlocked it. The gunman grabbed her arm.

"Don't fight me. You're coming along for the ride. Insurance." His voice trembled. This was not what he had been told. *A simple extraction. No fuss, no one gets hurt.*

"Your van is blocked in; you can't escape using a vehicle. The only way is across the fields and they are muddy. Give up." Sally tried to reason with him but his fight or flight instinct had kicked in. He was going to make an escape and take a hostage.

"I don't care, you're coming with me." He pulled open the door and pushed Sally out first, holding onto her arm. She screamed. In the yard, Sam appeared from the edge of the barn. He stopped when he saw Sally and the gunman.

"Back off!" The gunman aimed at Sam's head. "No one needs to die today!"

"Which way?" He shook Sally's arm "No tricks"

"Turn right, head right of the bonfire; follow the path to the field on the right." She spoke loudly to ensure that Sam heard. He looked on, terrified that his wife was about to lose her life. *This is all my fault,* he thought, and felt powerless to change anything. The gunman pushed Sally forward and followed her through the edge of the crowd away from the main event. Sam suddenly awoke from his trance. *That's not the quickest way to another exit. That leads to the building site. She's leading him away from the crowds. He'll be stuck on the building site.*

The three NPSA officers appeared from the other side of the barn. One went straight upstairs to arrest the intruders, the other two made their way towards Sam.

"He's taken my wife hostage." His voice trembled, but he managed to point in the direction where they had gone. "I think she is leading him onto the building site, She's trying to trap him or get him lost. Please help her!" Sam's last plea revealed his distress and anxiety. What had he done?

The two NPSA officers nodded and headed off in pursuit of Sally and the gunman.

Sally had indeed thought to misdirect the gunman and lead him away from the crowds but also into the darkness and danger of the building site where the new toilet block foundations and drainage pipes were in the process of being laid.

Sally walked as fast as she could, being pushed and shoved by the masked gunman. Very quickly, they melted into the gloom of the night. The glow of the bonfire gave less and less light as they stumbled towards the adjoining field that was to be the glamping site. Darkness closed in around them, and more than once they both fell, tripping on tufts of grass or slipping on the muddy rutted ground. An explosion made Sally jump and the gunman automatically crouched down. Suddenly the sky filled with red and green sparkles. Another explosion followed. The fireworks had started. The gunman gave a sardonic smile.

"Now no one will know if I have to shoot you." He could only just see her. He gripped her arm tightly. "No tricks. Show me the way to the road, then I let you go." They picked their way across the field towards the treeline on the other side. The tall trees devoid of any foliage silhouetted on the night sky made the dark blue horizon look like it was cracked.

"It is through the metal fencing. That is the edge of the site. The road is right on the other side of the trees." Sally could just about see the temporary metal fencing that contractors used to protect sites. "Keep going, we are nearly there, I promise." There was a desperate edge to her voice.

"Stop!" The gunman hissed. "Listen." Sally stood still listening. The noise of others following could be heard. Stumbling in the dark. No phones or torches to give away their location.

"They're coming for you. The police. If you want to get away, you have to hurry. They were already at the event. Crowd control." She tried to make it sound believable. Hoping the man with the Eastern European accent didn't know too much about policing in the UK.

He swore and turned towards the fencing. "You first." He pushed her forward. They stumbled on, Sally waiting for her chance. The closer to the fence they were the more likely her plan would work. They almost crashed into the fence it had become so dark. He pulled the fencing apart and they slipped through. The gunman turned back towards the lights of the bonfire and fireworks. He saw two silhouettes of men slowly making their way toward them. As he raised his gun to fire, he let go of Sally's arm to steady himself on the uneven ground. This was her chance. She shoved him as hard as she could. His feet gave way on the slippery, muddy ground and he fell on his back. As he did so, the pistol fired into the air and then he dropped it as he struggled to get a grip. He swore loudly in an Eastern European language as he scrambled to recover the gun. Sally took her chance and dived into a trench she knew would be there. It was about four feet deep. She landed in a muddy puddle and nearly choked. She commando crawled away down the trench into the darkness, then stopped and allowed herself to sink a little into the quagmire. She lay still and silent.

Swearing loudly in his native tongue, the gunman eventually managed to get up, his clothes face and hands covered in mud. His gun was lost. He turned to see the two police officers closing in rapidly, crouching to make themselves a smaller target. He turned back from the fencing and made straight for the tree line across the dark expanse where Sally had told him the road to safety was. He stepped forward cautiously not wanting to fall again. His arms out in front to steady him. He could hear the police officers closing in.

"Stop, MI5! This is your only warning!" The voice from the darkness behind him made the gunman hesitate just for a second. He made a split-second choice and decided to make a run for it.

MI5, what the f... he never even finished the thought. He fell headlong into what felt like oblivion. With a loud squelch, he landed facedown into the trench dug for the foundations of the toilet block. He tried to get up but the recent rain had turned the bottom of the eight-foot-deep trench into a sticky bog. The more he tried to move the more entrenched he became. With a loud curse, he gave up, his energy sapped. At that moment, two torch beams flicked on and scanned the area and the silhouetted figures of the MI5 officers stood atop the trench. He raised his hands in surrender, mud slowly dripping from his saturated clothing.

Sally dared not move. She was certain the gunman would try to find her. She listened carefully trying to gauge what was happening. She heard a splash and hoped that her plan had worked. Still, she lay quietly in the mud. After what seemed like an age, she saw torch beams scanning the ground and voices calling. One in particular resonated and filled her body with relief.

"Sally, where are you? Are you okay? It's safe to come out. We got them all. John is safe!" Sam sounded anxious; there was a tremble in his voice. As fast as she was able to, she heaved herself up from the shallow ditch and called out. "Over here! I'm okay Sam, I'm okay!" Three or four torch beams swung around and illuminated her muddy frame.

"Bloody hell, Sal, have you been mud wrestling?" It was a stupid thing to say but Sam was so relieved his wife was alive that the emotion flooded out as humour. He ran over to her and hugged her. She responded in kind and they kissed what turned out to be a very muddy kiss.

FORTY-SIX

In the farmyard, two police cars arrived and the three gunmen were arrested. Sally, Sam, and the others watched as the MI5 officers handed over the handcuffed men along with film footage taken by Ian's phone from the kitchen and Sally's from inside the shop. It was damning. A CID officer named Thompson took initial statements and invited them to Eastbourne police station the following day to make formal statements. Christos wandered over to one of the NPSA officers and ushered him back to where Sam stood.

"This is Mark Savage, he is an old friend, and we have worked together many times. He wants to hear your story."

After two hours, Mark Savage stood up from the kitchen table and shook Sam's hand. The two other officers did the same.

"If there is anything else you have that could give us a concrete link between Digamma and terrorist activity, anything on Frost or Chambers." He paused and shook his head, "I still struggle to believe that the PM's Aide and a major TV presenter could be involved in this."

"It's not just them. If Digamma and The Six are the same, then the four other trustees named on their website are also involved. They are all high-profile people." Sam was keen for them to understand how deep this went.

"I get it!" said Savage, "When this gets out, the shit really will hit the fan! I'll take it to the Director General, to see if it tallies with other intelligence we have. I'll be in touch."

By the time Savage and his team left, the bonfire party was winding down. Most of the locals had gone. The last of the hardy drinkers were still at the makeshift bar, and the bonfire was glowing like the site of a massive meteor strike. Only a few frightened customers in the shop and Sally's staff knew there had been an incident at all. In many ways, it had been a successful evening.

"You were so brave and resourceful. I knew there was a reason I married you." Sam and Sally were in bed. It was late. Both had been on the receiving end of a trauma, more than they had anticipated when they agreed to Christos' plan. More so, Sally, who had endured the chase across the building site and time spent in a muddy ditch. Yet her resourcefulness had saved the day.

"I'm just glad no one got hurt, especially me! The people in the shop were stunned but it was over so quickly that they seemed not to realise the danger." Sally leaned in and kissed her husband. "I am glad you understood my plan, otherwise it could have been different."

"That's why we're a good team." He picked up his glass of scotch, a little nightcap he felt they both needed. She did the same, they clinked glasses, "To us, a good team!" said Sam. They both drank and then fell into each other's arms to celebrate their survival.

Robert Frost looked at the burner phone again. Still no message. It was getting late. *They should have checked in by now.*

"Stop worrying, I suspect they have been delayed getting to the hideout. What could go wrong?" Melanie Chambers lay naked next to Frost in his bed at the house in North London. Their alibi was secure; they were together all night. "Let's not waste the time we have alone." She turned his head towards hers with her hand and kissed him. He immediately felt the tingling sensation in his groin and responded.

FORTY-SEVEN

Frost awoke to find his bed empty. He could hear Melanie downstairs. The radio was on and the smell of breakfast wafted through the house. It was a picture of married bliss, except they were not married and Frost and Melanie were not in love. They used each other's bodies for pleasure; there was no romance involved. He got up and then remembered to check his burner phone. He picked it up, but there were still no messages.

"Shit!" He grabbed his clothes, dressed hurriedly and went downstairs. As he entered the large kitchen diner, Melanie turned to greet him. She wore jeans and a tight-fitting tee shirt that said 'I love science.' It had a symbol of an atom underneath. She passed him a plate of bacon sandwiches.

"There's a pot of coffee on the table." Frost sat down and poured himself a mug of coffee.

"There is still no message from the team. Something must have gone wrong." Melanie sat down opposite and bit into a sandwich. She looked at Frost and could see the anxiety building on his face.

"Perhaps they double-crossed you? Took the money and ran. After all, they were just cheap gangsters. Why don't we head out to the rendezvous point as planned, and see what occurs? Maybe the phone was lost in the kidnap. Maybe they're waiting there right now." She tried to sound calm, but deep down she felt a knot developing in her stomach. "Eat your breakfast and then we can head out to the rendezvous." She looked at the clock on the wall. "We have plenty of time. I need to shower and dress properly. Wanna join me in the shower?" Despite the tension and anxiety of the situation, Melanie could not contain her base instincts. She ran her tongue over her top lip seductively to encourage Frost to respond.

"Most definitely, but first I need bacon. You always seem to put things in perspective, Mel." He bit into his sandwich with gusto; the façade of Robert Frost, Prime Minister's Aide, was all gone. He was Bobby the hormone-fuelled teenager who desired food and sex above all else.

The rendezvous point was an empty factory site on a derelict industrial estate in East London, south of the Thames near Woolwich. It used to be a factory of some sort, but now it was wild, nature reclaiming the site and the evidence of graffiti and vandalism was everywhere. As Frost and Melanie Chambers pulled up in his Jaguar, carefully avoiding the detritus and potholes they noticed small fires burning and groups of homeless people crowding around. Several of them turned to gawp at two strangers clearly out of their comfort zone and home territory.

"I hope you have a bloody gun!" Melanie demanded, her eyes taking in the scene. "I don't fancy getting out of the car without one."

"Of course I have. In the bag on the back seat. One for you as well. Maybe we could do some target practice right here, in case we need to dispose of Tucker and his wife. Or even the damn immigrant gangsters we employed. If they ever show up!" Frost spoke in a matter-of-fact tone and at first Mel thought he was kidding, until she saw the steely look in his eye. She leaned over, picked up a small sports bag, and placed it on her lap. Unzipping it she pulled out two Glock automatic pistols and then one that looked like a small machine gun. She had never seen one like it before. There were several cartridges of ammunition in the bag as well. Her eyes widened in disbelief.

"You weren't kidding were you Rob? Where did you get it all? Are you intending to use them or are they just for show?"

"It was part of the price I paid to our Eastern European friends. If they have double-crossed me, then at least I can kill them with their own weapons." He picked up one of the pistols and played with it in his hands, weighing it up. He raised the pistol and held it against Melanie's head.

"One click and you're gone. You'd better be a good girl." His grin seemed evil and his eyes empty of emotion.

"Robbie, stop! You're making me uncomfortable." Beads of sweat appeared on her forehead and ran down the side of her face. Keeping the gun at her head, he spoke softly.

"Have you ever killed anyone, Mel? I mean not ordered their death or planted a bomb. But right up close. You know, pulled the trigger, or plunged the knife in?"

"N...no, no.... I haven't." Her feeling of discomfort increased. Frost's tone had changed. He was distant as if his emotions had shut down. The man she slept with was gone, hidden deep inside him. This was an even more basic version of Robert Frost. She wasn't fearful of her life but this was a new side to him she had not yet experienced.

"I have," he said slowly and without emotion. "I killed my father, the selfish, cold-hearted pompous bastard that he was. It made me feel strong and invincible; I have longed to do it again. It is the only time I was truly free of any restraint." His breathing increased in intensity as he recalled the events of the death of his father. Melanie listened with a mixture of shock and awe at his attitude. The pride in his voice, the sense of freedom she heard in his voice.

"I was true to the Atomist and hedonistic principle; doing what gave me pleasure and what was right in my own eyes." She slowly turned her head to face him, the barrel of the gun millimetres away from her skull. There was passion in his eyes, along with an absence of humanity. Carefully she raised her hand, placed it on the barrel of the gun, and lowered it from her face. She blew out her cheeks. She looked out of the car window and saw several homeless people dressed in dirty overcoats and shoes with holes in, unkempt hair and uncut beards, standing, watching the two strangers in the posh car, just sitting there.

A strange and new sensation filled Melanie chambers, one that both aroused her sexually and confused her. She caressed the barrel of her own gun, feeling its power and hidden energy. Frost looked at her and smiled.

"You feel it too." He smiled at her with his mouth only. It was cruel. He cocked the pistol, looked at his companion and spoke. "Shall we do some target practice?" They both slipped the pistols down the back of their waistbands and got out of the car. Leaving the doors open, they casually wandered over to the group of curious homeless men and women. There were about eight in all.

"Good afternoon," Frost spoke like a PM's Aide once more, the mask temporarily slipping back into place. "We represent a charity that wants to clean up our world, make it better, and improve life. We are here to give you something. It would give us both great pleasure if you would receive our gift." He smiled genially as did Mel, although her heart was racing and her groin ached. The curious crowd seemed to relax on hearing the message of hope. Their expectations rose, only to be dashed when both Frost and Melanie Chambers slipped the hidden pistols from their waistbands and opened fire. The first two fell instantly, blood exploding from their chests. The third and fourth tried to turn away but fell as bullets ripped into their sides. By now, the final four were trying to run away, but being as they were either high, drunk or incapable due to poor footwear, it was a simple job for Frost and Melanie to aim, fire, aim fire until all eight were dead. The gunshots echoed around the empty industrial estate. Birds suddenly rose into the air, frightened by the boom of the guns. Melanie stood over one body, his chest missing and blood spreading rapidly on the ground around him. He was clearly dead. The look of shock on his face upset Melanie, so she aimed at his eyes and pulled the trigger again. His head disappeared. Blood and brain matter splattered out and up onto Melanie. She squealed, half in shock half in delight. She and Frost moved around all eight corpses, offloading more bullets into the already dead bodies. Only when their guns were empty did they return to the car, breathing heavily, bloodied and both overly aroused. They stripped off their bloodied clothes and threw them onto the small fire that roared in appreciation. Standing there in their underwear they both began to laugh manically, madness filling their minds.

FORTY-EIGHT

Frost and Melanie spent the afternoon in bed, expending their sexual energy and reliving the excitement of the power they felt in taking so many lives at once. Gradually some semblance of sanity returned. It was in the late afternoon that Melanie flicked on the TV news channel in Frost's bedroom and saw the scrolling news headline.

A Sussex farm targeted by armed robbers- Three men arrested

"Shit, Bobbie, look!" Melanie pointed to the screen. Frost looked up from drying his hair after his third shower of the day. The colour drained from his face.

"Look it up on your phone. Find out what's going on. Find out if we need to act quickly." Mel snatched up her phone and scrolled down a national news app.

"Here it is," she scanned it quickly and then began to read. *"Three men were arrested at Downs Wood Farm last night (Nov 5th) after a failed armed robbery."* She looked up quizzically. *"The three men all from Romania, attempted to rob a farm shop during a local bonfire event. Sources say that they mistakenly believed there would be significant cash on site, not realizing the event was free. Police supervising the event apprehended them after the robbers failed to escape because a tractor blocked the only road out."* She looked up and shook her head.

"No wonder they didn't contact us, they cocked the whole thing up!" She scanned the rest of the story. "Listen to this," she continued the story. *"Event organiser, and owner of Downs Wood Farm, Sam Tucker said, 'It is lucky for us that we invited the local police to attend and display some of their vehicles for the children. We had several police officers on hand, including firearms officers.'* Lucky for them indeed." Mel stopped reading, noticing that Frost was not listening anymore. He picked up the burner phone used to communicate with the gang and pulled out the SIM card, bent it in half until it snapped, then dropped it in the waste bin. He stamped on the phone until it resembled a jigsaw. Rage burned in his eyes.

"I don't believe it," There was frustration and anger in his voice. "They know. They set us up." "If that's the case, why are we still here, surely we'd all have been arrested by now. As well as the other members of 'Six'." Melanie was uncertain; she didn't believe that Sam and Sally were that deceptive. "The Tuckers are blundering around in the dark, on some Agatha Christie goose chase."

"That may well be true, or we may have been played like fools. Either way, we need to alert the others. You take care of Europe I will notify the heads of the other regions." Melanie turned back to her phone and typed a message on their secret group chat.

> To all trustees, please be aware that one of our ventures has faced issues. As a trustee, you may need to take appropriate action.

The simple message would be deleted once read and no one could copy the message. The message itself if read by anyone else would be meaningless. It was standard procedure to protect themselves. Unfortunately, Melanie was unaware that Christos had cloned her phone when he broke into her flat, and every message was copied to Sam's server. Frost sent a similar message to the heads of The Six across the globe.

Frost sat down on the edge of the bed next to Melanie. "We have a choice. We either assume we are in the clear and that fool Tucker and his wife know nothing, meaning we continue as before. Alternatively, we go on the offensive, grab the man called Johnny Saint, dispose of Tucker and his wife and destroy the farm. Leaving us in the clear."

"Both options are risky." Melanie paused for thought. The

sensation of joy and freedom that swept through her when she killed the homeless men was one she wanted to repeat. She had been free, or so she thought, of all responsibility. Free to act on impulse, desire and self-gratification, pure hedonism. She had truly become an Atomist.

"I say we go for the second option. Better to be proactive than reactive. If you want a job done well, do it yourself." In her mind's eye, she visualised shooting the bitch Sally Tucker and her pretty friend Kelly. She wanted to see that farm burn. *Why should they have it all?*

"If we can prove that Johnny Saint is the real apostle, and he does fit the profile, we can kill him publicly and bring down the mighty religion of the Christians. The Bible will be proved wrong and the revolution of the Atomists will begin."

Robert Frost smiled as he listened to Melanie; she had really bought into the beliefs of Atomists. *She is truly amoral,* he thought, with some pride.

"Agreed," said Frost, "I will inform the others that our final stage plan is to be put into operation as of today. We will all meet tonight to finalise the plans" He leaned over and kissed Melanie on the lips, holding her head in his hands. "Are you ready? Ready to lead this nation into a new era of freedom and pleasure? Are you ready to be Queen of freedom and desire?" Her pupils dilated and her body tingled with excitement. She was ready.

FORTY-NINE

As the afternoon sun set, Sam and Christos sat in Sam's study, reviewing copies of the footage they had taken the night before that captured the actions of the three masked gunmen. Mark Savage, the MI5 officer, had worked closely with the local police to keep the story to one of armed robbery rather than kidnap, in the interests of national security. They were happy to oblige, as the footage of the men was enough to put them behind bars for several years.

"I still can't believe we pulled it off, it is just a pity we can't conclusively link it to Robert Frost and The Six." Sam was glued to the screens, watching the events unfold. He still had pangs of anxiety when he saw Sally being dragged off into the darkness by the masked gunman from the shop.

"Sally did really well," said Christos, sensing Sam's unease. "Anyone would think she had training. What she did last night was amazing." Christos saw the smile creep across his friend's face. "Savage has agreed to flag Frost, Chambers and the other four trustees of Digamma on the MI5 watch list. It means that any unusual activity, travel or contacts will be identified, monitored and followed up. It's all I could get him to do without further information or evidence."

"But in the meantime, they are free to plan another attack and maybe be more successful. They will know that we set them up to flush them out. I think we may have made ourselves a target." Sam spoke not realising the truth of his statement or the significance of what he had said, because he was simultaneously searching the folders on the server for any scrap of information that might help implicate Frost and Chambers and any of the other members of The Six.

"What's this folder?" said Sam quizzically, pointing at the screen to a folder named "Christos."

Christos leaned forward and nodded in recognition, "Ah that is the folder I created to store anything that came of Melanie's phone and Frost's laptop. It should have been storing everything they have done." There was a moment's silence while the two men processed what Christos had actually said.

"My God." said Christos with a sense of guilt, "I totally forgot I had done that. There must be something in here that will give us an edge on Frost." Sam turned to him wide-eyed and open-mouthed. He was about to chastise his friend when he clicked on a video file from Frost's laptop. It showed Frost, from behind sitting at a table and a large number of hooded figures, over thirty, sat around a long conference table, Frost's voice came over loud and clear.

"Ladies and Gentleman, thank you for giving up your time to attend the first of what I hope to be an annual gathering until our mutual quest is complete. The charity Digamma provides us with an excellent cover and we must ensure that remains intact and is reputable and law-abiding. Please continue to arrange, support and finance for a wide range of events that promote scientific and rational understanding of the planet. We must deflect any suspicion away from us at all times. In the meantime, whilst we are together we must plan for the downfall of religious beliefs of all kinds through terror, murder and political manipulation."

Sam and Christos looked at each other in surprise and an element of joy. "Bloody hell," said Sam to himself, "we've got them, we've got them all!" The clip continued, Frost still speaking. He had turned his head so the camera, wherever it was had him in profile.

"I believe it is time we dispensed with secrecy. I know it is an ancient tradition of the Atomists. But how can we enjoy each other's company and share in each other's pleasures if we remain unknown to each other? I propose we lower our hoods. The European sector has already done so. We are known to each other." They both watched the film clip unfold on screen. Members of Digamma lowering

their hoods and revealing their faces. It was all there.

"Look," Sam pointed at the screen. "There's Mel. My God, that's the Assistant Chief Constable of the Met, Thomas Dexter, and look Celia Hartington, and all the Digamma trustees are there. That's it, we have them." Sam almost jumped up from his chair in delight.

"There are prominent business people and celebrities from across the globe." Christos' eyes bulged in awe of how wide and deep the Atomist movement went. "This is huge, but we need more to convince Interpol to act on all these."

"I think we might just have it, listen."

Frost's voice continued. He was clearly the leader, although the Arab woman at the far end seemed to have authority as well.

"My fellow Atomists, our search for the Apostle John continues. I believe him to be alive and his whereabouts to be known by this man and his wife." Sam and Sally's faces appeared on the screen. Sam's face turned pale as he watched realising how dangerous this group actually were and how lucky he and Sally were to be alive. He continued to concentrate on ~Frost's voice.

"I will concentrate on this aspect of our mission with my European colleagues. Each of the other sectors must increase your activity tenfold to create as much chaos, unrest and mistrust as possible. I want the New Year to be a time of radical development for our cause. Increase attacks on religious buildings, lobby for restrictions of faith activities, and organise assassinations of key religious figures. I suggest we target the Pope, the Dalai Llama, the Archbishop of Canterbury, the leader of the Sephardi Jews and finally the King of Saudi Arabia. In terms of historic sites, we need to destroy the Dome of the Rock and make it look like Zionists were responsible. An attack on the Kaaba would be a challenge but well worth it. I expect we could blame American Evangelicals for that one!" They pressed pause and sat back in their chairs not quite believing what they had just witnessed.

"My God, we had this all along, we could have prevented last night from happening!" Sam turned to his friend.

"Never mind, my friend. There is more, we have enough to damn them all to the hell they don't believe in." Christos took the mouse and opened a file from Melanie's cloned phone. They sat for hours scanning through files and further video clips of Zoom meetings all of which heaped more coal on the fire that would burn down The Six and enable Johnny Saint to live in peace.

"We need to warn Johnny, get him out of here, somewhere safe. Frost won't stop until he's killed him."

"Agreed. I will take all this information to Savage personally, tonight. You, Sally and Johnny get away; hide somewhere. Tell Kelly and Ian to take a holiday until this is over."

FIFTY

Ian and Kelly reluctantly agreed to go. Sam booked them onto a flight from Gatwick to Madrid and made reservations in a small boutique hotel for a week.

"Enjoy a break, you deserve it. Now get going, your flight leaves in four hours." They hugged and saw them off the premises. It had been a struggle to get them to agree but Sally assured them that they too would be disappearing and that MI5 were doing the rest. As the Audi pulled out of the drive from Ian and Kelly's cottage Sam turned to his wife. "Now for the difficult job of persuading Johnny to take a holiday with us." She laughed.

"You're not wrong. He's a stubborn bloke. That apostle."

Sam turned to his wife as they walked back to the main farmhouse, Ronnie the dog scampering alongside them. "Do you think it is real? Is Johnny the apostle John?" He flicked on the torch he was carrying and the beam spread out in front of them lighting their way home. It was a clear and chilly night. The stars were visible directly above as was the orange glow that was Brighton to the west.

"If I was certain he was then I would have to believe the whole God thing, Jesus, the cross, the Bible, the whole lot. I am not sure I am ready for that, just yet."

Sam smiled at his wife, his love for her immense, more than he could express in words.

"I think it is him. We will find out soon enough when that DNA test comes back. Christos said it should be back soon."

"If it is him, will you become a Christian? It's a big step. It will change everything."

"Yeah, I know, but not in a bad way. Look at how content Johnny is. How sure of his life, his future. He has hope beyond his circumstances. He knows for sure, what he believes and lives by it."

"Maybe because he saw Jesus in the flesh, two thousand years ago. He knows it is true." Sally squeezed her husband's hand. "I hope it is him, I need that assurance. I know we have all the money in the world, a lovely life, a great home, excellent friends in Ian and Kelly, Christos and Maria, but…" Sally paused, not wanting to upset her husband. He interrupted her

"But you wonder if that is all there is? You want there to be more, but you are frightened to commit, in case you are wrong? You want proof!" Sally nodded in agreement.

"Me too. Johnny once told me that faith is being certain of what you cannot see. Or something like that. I think it was a Bible quote."

She laughed at his vague attempt at quoting the Bible. "So the Apostle John speaks words of wisdom and you can't even remember them." They ambled up the path that led to the farmhouse and farm shop. If they had been walking on the road rather than across the fields they would have seen a Jaguar parked in the lane just out of sight of the farm.

FIFTY-ONE

The lights were on in Johnny's apartment above the shop when Sam and Sally entered the farmyard. Ronnie raced off and into the boot room where his basket was. Sam watched him, noticing how cosy and warm his home looked from the outside. The curtains were drawn and light escaped from their edges giving the farmhouse a welcoming feel. He noticed wisps of smoke from the main chimney curling up into the night sky. *Thanks, Johnny, you set a fire for us.* His kindness and selflessness never ceased to amaze him. He assumed that Johnny's Christian faith made him more aware of serving others, or perhaps it was just his nature. Either way, he was glad Johnny was his friend and back in his life. They entered through the office staircase rather than going through the shop. When they got to the landing, they both noticed the door to the apartment was ajar.

"At least we know he's in," said Sally with relief.

"But it won't make our job any easier, convincing him that he is still in danger." Sam raised his eyebrows to emphasise the point. Johnny was a stubborn man. Sam pushed open the door and called out.

"Johnny, are you around, mate? Do you have ten minutes for a chat?" When they entered the sitting room, Johnny was sitting on one of the deep, comfy chairs, but facing the door. His expression was one of warning. Sally spoke first.

"What you doing? Why are you sitting like that, and what's with the face?" When Robert Frost stepped out from behind the door and spoke, both Sam and Sally jumped in surprise.

"Welcome to my party!" Frost stood pointing his Glock automatic pistol. Sam and Sally both turned in shock at the unexpected voice. At that moment, Melanie Chambers appeared from the kitchen, also wielding a Glock automatic. She smiled like a genial host.

"At last our final guests have arrived. Let the party begin." She said almost manically. Her pupils were dilated as if she were on some drug, but it was pure adrenalin, the excitement of another kill looming. Sam made to take a step forward. Swiftly, Frost straightened his gun arm and aimed directly at Sam's head.

"Don't even think about it Sam." Sam and Sally both raised their hands.

"Sam, Sally, just do as they ask. They want me. You will be fine if you let them take me." Johnny spoke calmly and in a way that actually made them both feel better. It was as if some other force were at play.

"Good advice from Saint John over there. Unfortunately, some of it is untrue." Frost smiled and this time it reached his eyes. His eyes revealed menace and madness. Melanie stepped forward.

"Yes, sadly for you Sam, we're going to kill your wife…" Sam tensed as if to rush forward and attack Melanie.

"Tsk tsk Sam, be a good chap and behave. I don't want to spoil our party by having to shoot you here."

"Don't spoil the fun Bobbie, I want to watch them squirm, then burn." Melanie Chambers laughed at her own rhyme, thinking it to be the funniest thing ever. Sam and Sally looked at each other, fear on their faces.

"Enough of this. Let's get this party started. Mel, get these two tied up. I was going to burn them in their own home; I even lit the fire ready, but let's do it here."

Mel picked up a coil of 6mm hemp rope that she had taken from the shop downstairs and threw it at Johnny. "Here you tie them up, nice and tight, no tricks. I'll check! Tie them back to back, so they can't even look each other in the eyes when they die!" The coil of rope landed on the coffee table in front of Johnny and skidded across it, knocking several items onto the floor. The rope fell to the floor in front of Johnny and behind the table out of sight.

"Well, get on with it, Johnny. Or should I say, Saint John?" She cackled, the last vestiges of reasonable behaviour disappearing.

"Robert, you won't get away with it! Christos has evidence that you are the head of The Six and you plan to assassinate several world leaders and desecrate religious sites. It's all over. We know who all the worldwide 'Six' are. He is on his way right now to MI5" Sam hoped this would make his old friend think again. "Robert we're old friends. You don't do this to friends."

"Friends!" he almost shouted. "You made your choice, all those years ago when you chose, him over me. You chose God over your friend. You chose the church instead of me." He pointed the gun at Johnny. "I needed a friend, I needed you. You betrayed me."

"I just went to a church youth club. You could have come too."

"After what that priest did to me, you think I would ever allow religion to harm me again." He was shaking. "I needed you to help me but you chose him."

"Is this what it is all about? The Six. Revenge for what a sick man did to you years ago. Do you think trying to rid the world of religion will make you feel better? You had a bad experience, so everyone has to suffer. You are mad!"

"You have no idea. The Atomist movement gives us all freedom, freedom to be who we want to be without the constraints of religion, binding us up." Frost's eyes were filled with madness, he was consumed by his beliefs, no better than a religious zealot killing in the name of God.

"What makes you so different from Bin Laden, Sinn Fein, the Taliban or even the good old crusaders a thousand years ago? You have just replaced religion with Atomist values. You're just a simple egoist who wants to rule the world his way. At least the God that I believe in speaks of love, compassion and forgiveness." He paused for breath. It took him a moment to realise what he had said, that he had professed belief in God. Sally stared at her husband and then looked at Johnny, who was busy picking up the detritus from the coffee table spillage. There in front of him was his penknife, the one he used every day around the farm.

"Come on Bobbie, don't listen to that feeble Christian, *'At least the God that I believe in speaks of love, compassion and forgiveness'*" Melanie mimicked Sam's voice, ridiculing his profession of faith. "Hurry up St John we haven't got all night. We have killing to do." She raised her pistol in an attempt to hurry him up. She turned to Frost and whispered.

"How does he know about the assassinations?" For a moment, there was concern in her voice.

"It doesn't matter now, the final stage has begun. All over the world, a new order is beginning, we have done it!" He kissed Mel briefly on the cheek and then turned to his captives.

"Get on the floor both of you, back to back!" Frost had regained control; the cold emotionless mask had fallen back into place. His childhood traumas pushed back down into the depths of his black soul. Johnny began to tie them up. Melanie shouted instructions.

"Make sure it's tight, cut off their circulation."

"You're mad, both of you," Sally spoke for the first time. She could not believe the madness she was witnessing.

"You're mad, both of you." Once again, Melanie mimicked the voice. "Aah, poor Sally, have you got the God bug too? Well, it's a good thing you'll be dead soon, you can meet him!" She cackled again.

As Johnny tied Sam's wrists behind his back and then intertwined them with Sally's tied wrists, he slipped the small penknife into Sam's palm. He closed his hands around it tightly. A swift glance between the two men was all that was needed by way of a thank you. Sam tried one last time.

"Robert, what are you going to do now? By now MI5 will have all the information they need to arrest you all. Where will you go? You can't seriously think you can kill Johnny here, claiming him to be a two-thousand-year-old apostle. You realise what that sounds like."

Frost knelt down in front of Sam whilst Melanie tied Johnny's wrists behind his back. She then pushed him down on the sofa.

"Wait there, Johnny boy. We're going on holiday. I've got your passport!" She picked up his passport from the coffee table and waved it in Johnny's face. He sat there and smiled politely.

Lord. Protect my friends, and give them what is needed to survive. He prayed silently whilst holding Melanie in his gaze. It unnerved her. She slapped him.

"Stop staring old man."

Frost momentarily looked up at Melanie, just as he was about to speak. The look on his face was like thunder. "Mel, be careful what you say!" He turned back to Sam, lying on the floor, trying not to strain against the ropes. If he strained it would be more uncomfortable for Sally.

"Look what I found in the bedroom drawer." He held up a pair of socks. Before Sam could object, he stuffed a sock in Sam's mouth.

"Leave my husband alone you bloody freak!" Sally began to wriggle but soon stopped as she heard he husband's muffled cries. Her movement caused her husband pain.

"That's it lay still. Open wide." He held the gun at her head. She obeyed. He stuffed the other sock in her mouth. She tried to object but the force was too great, she nearly choked.

"Now before we go, let me tell you this. Johnny here will die, very publicly. MI5 will not find us because within the hour we will be out of the country. The Six will continue its mission, religions worldwide will crumble, and I will become the one who leads this nation into a new hedonistic future, where pleasure reigns supreme. I am the saviour this world needs, not your ancient Son of God, Jesus." He stood up and turned to leave, then turned back.

"Ah Sam, I almost forgot, I've wanted to do this since the first time I met your wife." He leered down at Sally. Her eyes widened with fear. He knelt beside her, Sam straining his head to see what Frost was doing. He tried shouting obscenities at Frost but the sock made it impossible.

"Keep still, my lovely." Slowly his hands untucked her tee shirt and he slipped his left hand up under her bra. Sally wriggled to try to escape.

"Now, now." Frost pressed down on Sally's shoulder with his right hand, the butt of the pistol pressing down on her shoulder. The pain was intense and she had no option but to relax. He continued to massage her breast.

Hatred and rage consumed Sam and he tried to stop Frost by wriggling and kicking out but his body would not move.

"Still filled with love and compassion, Sam? Or has that turned to hate? See, your God is false; the only truth is our basest instincts. So why not embrace them." He stood up and kicked Sam in the stomach. Pain seared through Sam's body bringing tears to his eyes.

"So long, Sam Tucker and his beautiful wife, you will soon be dead. I would say, you will meet your maker, but I don't believe there is one." He grabbed Johnny, hauled him up out of the sofa and pushed him through the door.

Melanie took one last look at Sam and Sally trussed up like Christmas turkeys lying on the floor and closed the door behind her. That action would ultimately save Sam and Sally's life.

FIFTY-TWO

Sam lay still. He knew Sally was crying. The strained coughs through the sock stuffed in her mouth and the shaking of her shoulders made it clear. He could hear noises downstairs in the shop as Frost and Melanie Chambers planned their death. Sam felt something in his palm and remembered the object Johnny had slipped him. Working it in his fingers, he recognised its shape. His eyes lit up with hope. *Johnny, you are a saint.* He needed to breathe properly, to speak Sally, comfort her, rescue her, and hold her close. He was determined that he would escape. Frost had been in such a hurry that his attempt at silencing Sam had not been as good as it should have been. Sam had closed his mouth around the sock before it all was in his mouth; Frost had not noticed or had not thought it important. Ultimately, it meant that he could still move his tongue. Opening his mouth, he began to work the sock out of his mouth. His tongue ached, and his jaw screamed in agony as he tried to push the sock forward and expel it from his mouth. After several minutes, the sock fell from his mouth and he gulped in air filling his lungs. Sally began to wriggle, realising something had changed.

"Sal, Sally, are you okay?" It was a stupid thing to say, she clearly wasn't but he could not think of anything else.

"Mmmm…mmm…mm" He took that to mean that she was.

"Listen, when Johnny tied us up he slipped a penknife into my hands, I think together we could open it and cut the rope. It's not very thick." He could feel Sally's fingers searching for the knife and then exploring it.

"Mmmm…mmm."

"I'll open it. We may get hurt but it's the only way." He rotated the knife in his hands and picked at the blade with his fingernail. As he finally opened the knife and Sally ran her finger across the blade to discover the way it was facing, Sam heard sounds outside the door. A crackling sound like fire. He turned his head to see tiny wisps of smoke filtering under the door. An explosion and the sound of shattering glass made them both jump. The knife stabbed Sam, pricking his skin.

"Ouch! Shit, they have set the shop on fire. We have to work fast." The mumbled response from Sally held even more fear. They began working at the ropes with the knife, jumping in pain each time they missed and hit flesh. Muffed squeals from Sally and cries of pain from Sam continued as the sound of the shop burning continued below them. Sam could feel the heat in the floor from the raging inferno below. Blood began to ooze from their tied hands making it difficult to grip the knife. They could hear Robbie barking in the yard, wondering where they were.

The ropes began to split strand by strand, and the binding loosened. Both of them were sweating with the heat and the effort of their work. Smoke filtered under the door, rising to the ceiling. Alarms were ringing and Sam prayed that the sprinklers had gone off to quench the flames.

"Come on Sal, we can do this, I am not going to die here! We are not going to die here!" He coughed as he spoke, the smoke becoming thicker. The paint on the door to the lounge was bubbling; the flames were in the flat itself. He silently thanked God for building regulations and fire doors, but he knew by the gagging noises his wife was making that she was near exhaustion and overcome by smoke. With one final effort, he thrust the knife forward and upward with all his might and began sawing at the rope. He screamed as it tore into his flesh as well. He felt Sally wriggle to escape the pain.

"Lord, please!" He screamed the prayer. The ropes gave and his hands fell free. He collapsed, dropping the knife. Freeing his hands from the tangle of the ropes, he tried to remove the sock from Sally's mouth but he could not reach it. He realised her hands were still tied. Groping again for the knife he cut his feet free and turned to remove the sock from his wife's mouth. She coughed and spluttered gulping in smoky air, making her cough further. Slicing through the remaining cords, he grabbed his wife and dragged her across the room toward the fire exit door. All around, the glow of the fire below was engulfing the building. He pushed open the fire exit, picked up his wife in a firefighter's lift and carried her down the fire escape. Only when they reached the safety of the farmhouse did he lay her down on the kitchen table. The adrenalin seeping away replaced by lactic acid. His limbs felt heavy, and his breathing laboured but they were safe. Robbie ran around barking frantically tail wagging.

"Sally, Sally," There was fear in his voice. She coughed and spluttered then gulped air into her lungs.

"What took you so long?" She smiled up at her husband. "Now get me a bloody drink. I'm parched!" The sound of sirens broke the moment as two fire engines and an ambulance appeared in the yard.

FIFTY-THREE

They sat in the kitchen. A paramedic packed away the first aid kit whilst another made tea. Their hands were bloodied and cut, but by the grace of God, no arteries had been cut or neither of them would have survived.

A firefighter entered the kitchen, holding her helmet under her arm. She smiled.

"You're lucky to be alive, a great deal of accelerant was used, that's why it took so quickly. Fortunately, your sprinkler system worked well and dampened everything, slowing its progress. It is mainly superficial, but we will do a full report for your insurance company. This was definitely arson."

At that moment, Christos, Mark Savage and Thompson the CID officer walked in.

"My God, look at you," said Christos shocked at the bandages on the hands of his friends. He stepped over and hugged them both.

"We have an all ports warning out for Frost and Chambers. Photographs are being circulated." Savage was taking control. "They won't get far."

"They have John as hostage. They will kill him." The tone of Sam's voice, albeit husky from the smoke, made Savage stop in his tracks. "He is what they want. Once they are sure he is the apostle, they will publicly prove it and then execute him. They won't go abroad, Frost wants to start a revolution here, not in Europe. The passport and going abroad talk was insurance in case we escaped."

Savage raised an eyebrow, "What makes you so sure?"

"Just a feeling." Sam shrugged.

"Intelligence agencies from around the world are using the information we shared. In a few days, we will have them all. The

Six is dead." There was a note of pride in Savage's voice. Then he spoke again. "Thanks to you we have uncovered a global plot to undermine the world economy and political systems. Whatever you think of God and religion, we are all different and must learn to live together, whether we agree or disagree."

"Can you track them via their phones or car? Can't we use ANPR to track them?" Sally, having begun to recover from the effects of the smoke, was keen to see some action.

"It's all in hand. They have stopped using their phones and his car was last picked up on the M23 heading north."

"Have you searched his house?" Christos chipped in.

"They won't go there," Savage responded.

"No is his laptop there? We can track his laptop every time he uses it and connects to a phone signal. His laptop has 4G. He will still believe all the other sectors will be operating. He will want to contact them."

"Shit, you're right!" Savage picked up his phone and put the call through. "They're watching his house, I've told them to break in and find his laptop."

Five minutes later, Savage received the news he was waiting for.

"He has his laptop on him. It's not in the house! We need that laptop. We cannot use the footage you gave us in any trial, because it was obtained 'illegally.'" Savage made speech mark signs with his fingers and grinned. "We must have that laptop before he wipes the drive or destroys it." Savage turned to Sam; "Can we track his movements from your office? It will be quicker than getting back to London. It will give us a head start."

With a big smile, Sam spoke. "Definitely. This bastard burned my barn and nearly killed my wife. Use anything you like!"

FIFTY-FOUR

Frost drove all evening, only stopping to fill up his car. He was aware of ANPR cameras and knew the police and MI5 would be tracking him. Sam's comment about The Sixs' plans had shaken him. He knew it was true. He needed to get off the main roads. John was bound and gagged and lay in the back seat of the Jaguar. So far, he had cooperated but Frost couldn't help thinking it wouldn't last. Melanie rode shotgun, literally cradling her Glock automatic pistol, occasionally turning to check on their prisoner in the back. After the first stop for fuel, at Cobham Services, when she was recognised and had to play the part of 'Melanie Chambers, celebrity journalist' she chose to remain hidden in the car.

"You need to change your appearance. I bought you some hair dye and a sharp pair of scissors to cut your locks off." He threw a bag of goods on the back seat at John's feet. "Once we get off the main roads they can't track us and I know a place we can hide for a few days."

"Where are we going, Bobbie? I thought we were going to France."

"A false trail to slow down the enemy. However, I don't think it worked. Sam's description of our plans suggests our cover is blown. MI5, the police and anyone else with a conscience will be looking for us now." There was a tension in his face as he drove on late into the night.

"Open my laptop, get up Google Maps and find a way to get to West Witton in the Yorkshire Dales without using main roads. My darling late wife's family have a cottage outside the village. It's a holiday home. It will be empty, isolated and perfect to lay low."

"Sir, they've just passed Doncaster on the A1 according to ANPR." The voice over the phone on Savage's mobile was on speaker for all to hear.

"I want local police informed to track and trail but not intercept his car. I want to know where he's going."

Sam turned away from his bank of computer screens and spoke up. "He's going here," and pointed to a large display on Google Maps. There was a dropped pin in a village called West Witton near the town of Leyburn in North Yorkshire.

"How the hell do you know that?" Savage blurted out.

Christos smiled a smug smile. "He's turned on his laptop. Remember it has 4G. This has just been uploaded to Sam's server."

"Savage picked up his phone and spoke to the voice on the other end.

"I need to know, where exactly he is. What is there in West Witton? Why there?"

"Yes sir," said the disembodied voice. "Back ASAP."

Savage turned to leave, "Right I'm off, it's a long drive to Yorkshire from here and I need to assemble a team. Thank you, Sam, Christos. You have served this country well and done a fantastic job." He held out his hand for them to shake.

"Hang on a bloody minute," said Sam indignantly. "If you think you're going without me and Christos, you've got another thing coming. You'd have nothing without us."

"Agreed, we would, but you are civilians. I can't take you into a dangerous hostage situation."

"Too late for that. My wife was kidnapped by a gunman, we were nearly burned to death, and we've been embroiled in a global terror … something or other…" Sam struggled for the right word.

"Okay okay." Savage held up his hands in surrender. "But you stay in the cars out of sight.

"Sam!" He turned to see Sally staring at him, steel in her eyes.

"If you're going to try and stop me... then don't" There was similar steel in his voice.

"I'm not. Get the bastard and make him pay." She kissed him on the lips, a long lingering kiss that made the rest of the room uncomfortable. Sam smiled at his wife. He always did.

FIFTY-FIVE

By sundown the following day, a team of anti-terrorist police officers led by MI5 agent Mark Savage, sat in a function room of one of the several pubs in Leyburn the nearest town to the village of West Witton, four miles away. There had been no word yet about where in West Witton, Frost was headed. The laptop was off and had been for several hours. There was no way to triangulate a more precise setting. Sam sat nervously on the edge of an old wooden chair, one of four placed around an oak table that bore the scars of a hundred years of use. His muscular frame looked uncomfortable waiting for the action to begin. He brushed a hand through his thick brown hair and sighed heavily. Christos on the other hand was used to waiting. He was content messaging his wife back in Patmos. He missed her and his son Thomas. He longed to be home, in the warmer climate rather than the damp, dull English winter. It was sunny and eighteen degrees in Patmos. Time passed slowly, the team of twelve anti-terror police officers were fully armed and ready to jump into three vans. Savage paced the room like a caged tiger, occasionally stopping to study the large OS map of the area as if it would inspire him. His phone buzzed and everyone in the room looked up.

"Savage," he barked into the phone. He strode over to the map spread out over the table and studied it. "Yep, yep, got it, ok." He picked up a biro with his other hand and circled a section of the map. The conversation continued for a minute more before he ended the call and smiled a big smile that reached the sparkle in his eyes.

"Got them!"

There were positive exchanges around the room and Sam leapt to his feet and stepped over to the map. Christos followed, his black beard parting to reveal a big grin.

"Where are they?" Sam leaned over the map almost obstructing Savage's view.

"They are in a cottage owned by his late wife's family. It's a holiday home only used in the summer. It's always shut down in winter. So if there is anyone there, it's them!" Savage spoke with some degree of excitement. Sam looked at the circle drawn on the map. He clicked open his phone and found Google Maps.

"It's an isolated building off Green Gate at the far end of West Witton. It's up into the hills. Maybe a barn conversion. If it is a holiday home." Savage smiled at his enthusiasm and gently took control.

"Gather round," he gestured to the assembled team and began setting out a plan, taking ideas from other experienced officers until what appeared to be a practical plan for taking all three people alive was formulated.

FIFTY-SIX

"How do you like my new look?" Melanie made a show of twirling around in the living room of the small two-bedroomed barn conversion. It was well furnished in a modern style and had a satellite television and a shelf full of novels so they could pass the time in relative peace. Frost had turned on the heating rather than light a fire, which would draw attention from any locals passing by. They had stopped in Leyburn and bought a week's worth of provisions, ready to sit it out until Frost could organise an escape for them all using the faithful supporters of The Six whom he had often used for the more unsavoury jobs, such as arson, vandalism, and even murder.

"Well, what do you think of it?" Melanie gave a second twirl. She had cut her hair short and done her best to self-style it into a pixie look. Her hair was now brown and she resembled Emma Watson in her post Harry Potter era. Both men in the room looked up, Frost from his laptop where he was trying to access a secret email account which he used to contact his 'operatives'. However, the 4G signal was poor and there was no WiFi.

"Yeah great! You look lovely." There was no sincerity at all; he was too preoccupied.

"What about you St John? What do you think? Gorgeous or what?" Johnny sat on the sofa his hands and feet tied. He was trying to read a book. Frost had permitted him to have his hands tied in front of him, rather than behind, for him to be able to feed himself, drink and read books. He looked up and very deliberately said, "What?"

A cloud came over Melanie, "Well, thanks a lot boys. Here I am stuck in this miserable dump, with two men who don't appreciate a beautiful woman." She wandered over to Frost and leaned over his shoulder. "You're too interested in your bloody laptop to want to take any notice of me." She looked over at Johnny who was watching her now with interest, realising she did not like being ignored. "And he's Jesus' best friend so he's going to be no fun. I expect he still a virgin, even after two thousand years!" She laughed manically at her own joke. Johnny took his opportunity to throw some doubt into her mind, and maybe Frost's too.

"Why do you think I am some sort of apostle? You said 'Jesus' friend' What did you mean?"

"Come off it Jonny boy, we all know the truth." She sat down beside him and put her feet up on the coffee table. "You are in fact, St John, the apostle of Jesus who cannot die until Jesus returns. We've done our research; Johan Heiliger, Johhny Saint and all the other aliases. You've been wandering this earth for two millennia, helping the poor, serving your God, and being mister nice guy. We've been on your trail for a long time. The file on you is this thick going back centuries." She gestured with her hands to indicate a large file. Frost looked up from his laptop, closed the lid and sat back to join in. He picked up his Glock and pointed it at Johnny.

"Admit it, Johnny, it's the easiest thing in the world. Just a few simple words. Or I kill you now."

Johnny waited a moment and then smiled.

"Excuse me for being a little dense here. I have clearly missed something. If I am John the apostle, then you won't kill me. You can't kill me, because, if I am he, I cannot die. Therefore, your plan to execute me publicly to prove Christianity is false will obviously fail. If I am not John and you shoot me, I will die. In which case you have totally blown your cover for nothing. You will be on the run with nowhere to go. Stuck in the middle of Yorkshire with the body of some nobody called John. Have I got that right?" There was almost a smirk on his face by the time he finished speaking.

"Shut it, Johnny," Frost became suddenly angry. "I know what you're trying to do. Divide us, sow seeds of doubt. It won't work." He stood up and began pacing the room. He was agitated.

"Hey, Bobbie, it's fine. We know he is the one. He's just trying to bluff." She patted Johnny's cheek. "Aren't you Johnny baby?" She spoke in the tone of a mother patronising her children.

"You realise," said Johnny calmly, "that what you have both got to have is faith. That thing you hate so much. You have to believe; otherwise, you are lost. You will have no hope."

"I said shut up!" Frost stepped across the room in a flash and struck Johnny in the face with the side of his Glock. Johnny collapsed back into the sofa, unconscious, a big welt forming on the side of his head.

Melanie jumped up, "What did you do that for? He's just winding us up." Frost grabbed her; his passions aroused and kissed her full on the lips. She responded quickly realising she needed to take her chance for physical satisfaction before Frost's logical side took over. She began fumbling at his trousers. He picked her up in his arms and carried her into the bedroom.

Savage, Sam and Christos drove slowly past the cottage. It was pitch black, it was almost three in the morning and there were no stars or moon to light the way. There was no smoke from the chimney; the curtains were drawn but small chinks of light escaped from beneath the curtains.

"They're here," Savage said over his radio. "All units into position and await further instructions." Two black Transit vans moved off from the village of West Witton, one remained parked in the small carpark behind the Old Vicarage Hotel. Fifteen minutes later all units were in position. One van blocked the road back into the village to the east of the barn, about 500 yards from the cottage itself. The other blocked the southerly end of the road where it met a B road called High Lane. The barn was about 20 metres above the village in the dales. The road it was on was single track. One way in, one way out. Four officers approached the barn through the fields from the east and north, four others from the south and west. Savage, Sam and Christos sat in a 4x4 Range Rover alongside the van to the east, nearest the village.

"All units report in," Savage whispered into the radio. "Monitoring stations only. I repeat, monitoring only. Do not engage. We wait until we can actually see daylight before we move." Fortunately, for the officers out in the fields, the thick cloud cover kept the temperature at about ten degrees. At least it wasn't raining anymore.

FIFTY-SEVEN

As the first inklings of dawn began to appear in the sky, the outline of the cottage slowly became clear in the darkness. The armed police officer crept slowly towards it using every available point of cover to hide his approach. Reaching the cottage itself, he pressed himself up against the wall next to one of the windows. Slipping a small receiver from his utility belt, he stuck it to the corner of the window. In the 4x4 the receiver crackled into life. Sam jumped with a start. He had been sleeping. He stretched and looked around him. Savage listened intently through a set of headphones. Christos stared out of the window watching the day slowly arrive.

The armed officer sidled around the cottage keeping close to the wall until he came to the next window, adjacent to the front door. The curtains were not fully drawn and this time he placed a tiny camera onto the window in the gap where an image of the room was possible. In the Range Rover, the tablet came to life revealing the interior of the lounge. Sam leaned forward from the back seat and saw his friend Johnny lying on the sofa asleep, tied hand and foot.

"Visual contact made, hostage visible, but no one else. Maintain watching brief only. Try to get a camera in the bedroom. We need to see Frost and Chambers." Savage issued the order quietly through his radio. A whispered affirmative came crackling back.

The sound of someone using the bathroom came through the receiver.

"Someone is awake and moving around," whispered Savage. Sam looked at his watch. It was 6:30 a.m. "We need to get this done before the farm traffic starts moving and the school run begins."

"No visual available in the bedroom." The voice whispered into Savage's ears.

"Affirmative. Prepare for action in 10 minutes. Plan A. all units acknowledge."

Melanie Chambers left the bathroom, her hair wet from the shower. She wrapped the towel around her; it just about covered her decency. Not that she cared, her body was her temple and she enjoyed others seeing it and using it for their pleasure and hers. She sauntered into the lounge toward where Johnny lay on the sofa, carrying her clothes. She wanted to show that damn God freak what a woman looked like. She wanted him to want her. She needed him to respond to her. Everyone did, and he would too.

She knelt in front of Johnny and tapped him gently on the cheek to wake him.

"Bloody hell look at this!" Savage's voice filled the car. Christos and Sam looked over at the tablet. There was Melanie Chambers, practically naked, wrapped in a towel that just about covered everything.

"What's she doing?" They stared at the screen as if it was a peep show. Melanie sat Johnny up, rousing him from his slumber. She then dropped the towel to reveal her nakedness to him.

In the room itself, Johnny blinked several times trying to get the sleep from his eyes, not understanding what he saw. There in front of him was Melanie Chambers, naked. She was beautiful, with a body that any heterosexual man would desire.

"Hey, Johnny. Like what you see?" she posed for him, trying to get him to focus on her, to notice her beauty and respond.

"What? What are you doing Melanie? Why are you naked?" Johnny focused on trying to keep his eyes on her face. He knew what she was trying to do. He understood her base instincts.

"Come on Johnny, I know you want me. You must want me, everyone does." She stepped forward and sat astride him, facing him. She leaned into his face and whispered.

"Come on Johnny, give in to it. You know you want to." She began to gyrate on his lap trying to get him to respond. With all his might, Johnny focussed on other things. He was not going to let his deepest base instincts control him.

"Get off me, Melanie. I don't want you." It took every ounce of self-control for him to say it. He was, after all, a heterosexual man, and his body was naturally responding to stimulation. He repeated his request with more authority and this time used all his strength to push her aside. "Get off me, Melanie. I don't want you." She fell sideways and then back off the sofa onto the floor, arms and legs in all directions, nothing left to the imagination.

In the Range Rover, there was disbelief at what they witnessed.

"He must be a bloody saint, to resist that." Sam laughed as he watched Melanie tumble onto the floor.

"He's got more self-control than me. I'd have let her do whatever!" Savage said with a lecherous tone.

"Why was she doing that?" Christos asked, "What was the point?"

"I think," said Sam, watching Melanie scramble on the floor grabbing her towel and clothes and stomping off to the bedroom. "She is desperate to show that everyone is like her, responding to their base needs. She wants to justify her actions and her beliefs. She won't accept that some people have a different perspective on life."

Savage turned to face him. "Blimey, psychologist as well?" He grinned.

"No, the wise words of Johnny Saint!"

FIFTY-EIGHT

Melanie slammed the bedroom door and threw her clothes on the bed. Frost jumped up and grabbed his gun ready to shoot her.

"What the fu…" He stopped when he saw her naked rage.

"That monk Johnny won't have sex with me. He's a freak. Look at me Frost, who wouldn't want it?" She was genuinely upset, not understanding why someone would reject her offer of sex. Frost got out of bed and wandered over to Melanie. He kissed her on the forehead.

"This is why they all must die, Melanie. They are restricting our freedom, causing us pain. They do not bring joy to the world, but only rules that bind us. We need to be free of them all. Christians, Muslims, Jews, anyone who thinks that there is some God, giving orders that we must obey." He held her in his arms. "He'll be dead soon and you and I will rise to power, to set this nation free." He patted her bottom. "Now get dressed, it's nearly daylight. I'm taking a shower."

Melanie crossed the bedroom and pulled back the curtain to confirm Frost's words that it was nearly morning. The firearms officer was just scrambling back behind the garden wall by the road. Melanie's eyes widened; she pulled the curtain shut.

"Shit! Police outside. They've found us." Shouted Melanie. Frost froze in his tracks and then turned back.

"Quickly, get dressed; we have to get out." They dressed as fast as they could.

"Go, go, go. Plan A. Frost and Chambers are in the bedroom, Take them alive. Protect the hostage first. I repeat plan A." Eight armed officers began to approach slowly from the perimeter of the cottage, Crouching and seeking cover, expecting enemy fire.

The sun was just beginning to rise and break through the clouds. It looked like it might be a bright sunny day.

Frost, dressed in jeans, a jumper and a thick jacket, slung a backpack over his shoulder. He stood at the entrance to the lounge. Johnny Saint sat, hands and feet tied looking directly at him.

"Cheerio Johnny, this is not how it was supposed to end." He raised his Glock and pulled the trigger.

"There's been a gunshot from inside." The senior police officer spoke quickly. "Plan B full force."

Eight officers stood and ran towards the cottage, one carrying a red enforcer or 'Rammit'.

"Police! Police! Freeze! Stay where you are!"

The door to the cottage seemed to fly off the hinges, the officers burst through the door in an attack formation, ready to shoot.

"Hostage down! I repeat hostage down!"

"Clear."

"Clear."

"Clear." Came the voices from the radios as officers checked every room in the cottage. It was empty but for Johnny Saint and the police officers.

"Sir, they have disappeared." The voice sounded rightly concerned.

"That's impossible," said Savage angrily. "Search again. I'm on my way up." Savage turned to Sam and Christos. "Stay here by the van with these two." He pointed at the officers in the van parked next to them. "I can't risk you getting shot at." Reluctantly, Sam and Christos got out of the car and Savage drove off up to the cottage." It was fully light, but it was still cold and Sam shivered.

"Give me Patmos any day." Christos looked around at the bleak landscape, the winter dew on the land, the weak sunshine not having any impact and the breeze chilling him to the core.

"Where the hell are we and how did you know about it?" Melanie scrambled along a dark stone tunnel, her phone the only source of light.

"It was an escape tunnel, first used by the Royalists in the civil war. The barn was originally a barracks for Cavaliers. The tunnel was insurance in case of a Roundhead attack. Since then it's had a history of smuggling and most recently my late wife used it to sneak out into Leyburn when she was on holiday with her damn religious parents. She showed it to me the first time we stayed here." Frost scrambled his way through, crouching low so as not to bang his head. The tunnel emerged in a small stone storage barn one hundred yards across the field by the road. They pushed themselves up out of the damp, dark space and out into the cold, fresh Yorkshire air. A car raced up the road toward the cottage, a lone driver at the wheel. Frost smiled to himself, he had chosen his place of hiding wisely. He could imagine the confusion of the police, entering the cottage and finding Johnny Saint dead and no one else.

They crouched low and made their way along the hedgerow next to the road until they came to a black transit van blocking the road. Frost's eyes widened as he saw Tucker and Christos standing by the van. "I thought he was dead!" he whispered. His hand went to his pocket to pull out his Glock, but Melanie stopped him. She shook her head. "No, he can wait, we need to escape." Frost reluctantly agreed realising any further shots would bring the whole task force down on them. Moving further away, they stopped by a dry stone wall and crouched down.

"We need to split up. It will be quicker and safer." Frost opened his bag and gave Melanie her passport, a wad of cash and her Glock. "Make your way to Hull. We can get a ride to the continent and then make our way to Dubai. I have a contact there who will guide us to the head of the Middle Eastern 'Six.'" They kissed passionately and Melanie watched as Frost continued to run along beside the stone wall. Melanie looked both ways and hopped over the wall, crossed the road and climbed over a gate into a field on the far side. She had a plan. She would make her way to the Aysgarth Falls and then hitch a ride with some unsuspecting tourist. Maybe even hijack a car! The prospect was already exciting her.

FIFTY-NINE

"Where the hell did they go?" Savage was prowling the cottage. "People just don't disappear!" A police officer was performing first aid on Johnny Saint. "How is he?" said Savage, a look of concern on his face.

"He'll live. If the ambulance gets here quickly. We have one on standby in Leyburn rather than at the A and E in Darlington. He'd be dead if we had to wait for them." He continued to pack a wound and patch it up.

"He's lucky. Either Frost is a poor shot from short range or this guy fell to one side as the shot was fired. Either way, it missed his vital organs by millimetres."

"Sir look at this." Savage walked quickly down the hall to the bathroom. An officer was holding up a trap door in the cupboard that held the immersion heater and hot water tank. The tank was set two feet off the floor leaving a small floor space below which was covered by a rug. "I only noticed it when I saw the rug was ruffled and not laying properly."

"Well don't just stand there, take some men and see where it goes." Savage spoke brusquely.

Sam shivered again as the wind whistled up the road. There may have been some sun but it was bitterly cold. Something caught his eye, a movement in the reversing mirror of the transit. He turned around to see. About three hundred yards away he saw a figure walking briskly up the field away from the village. At first, he thought it was a dog walker, but then realised there was no dog. He stared intently, following her progress. Slowly, like the sunrise, it dawned on him. He tugged Christos's arm.

"Look," he whispered, pointing towards the figure. "That's Mel.

I'm sure of it." Christos went to tell the police officers, but Sam held him back.

"No. Give me your gun Christos. I know you have one. I'm going after her. That bitch burned my shop down and tried to kill my wife. She's probably killed Johnny too." At that moment, the sound of a siren drifted across the dales. The figure on the hill looked back, saw Sam and Christos staring at them, and turned and hurried on, increasing her pace.

"That's definitely her." Sam held out his hand waiting for Christos to give him his gun.

"You keep these guys occupied until I've got a head start."

"Just be careful, I don't want to be speaking at your funeral, my friend." Sam smiled.

"Got it. See you soon." Sam jogged down the road slipping the pistol into the back of his jeans.

He entered the field and began the long walk up the field. He followed her footsteps left in the dew. An easy trail, his mind recounting the ordeal by fire that Melanie had caused, the lies she had told him, her abuse of his friend, using her body to tempt him. *This woman is evil,* he thought. He stepped up his pace and reached the brow of the hill. He could see her at the bottom of the field on the other side. Climbing a gate. He called out.

"Melanie, stop! It's all over!" He couldn't be sure she had heard until he heard the crack of the pistol and he fell to the floor.

"Shit!" He crawled forward to the brow and peeked over. He could see her running across another field towards some trees. He got up and sprinted down the hill, tumbling as he neared the bottom to stop himself from crashing into the bushes. He was soaking wet with the dew from the ground. It was also slippy and sticky due to all the recent rain. He scrambled over the gate and continued the pursuit. Running as fast as he could, Sam began to catch up with Melanie. He saw her disappear into a wood. Another shot rang out and he felt the bullet whizz past his head. He crouched low and made his way to the edge of the field by a hedgerow that gave him cover. He waited, getting his breath back. He tried calling her again.

"Mel, this is crazy. You can't escape. Even if you kill me, it's all over." Another shot came his way followed by a stream of obscenities. Sam waited until it had gone quiet and all was still and then began a slow descent towards the woods where he thought Melanie was hiding. By the time he reached the woods, he could see her jogging towards some farm buildings and cottages.

"Shit, Mel, just stop!" He said to himself. He carried on towards the farm. By the time he arrived, a crowd of people was waving and screaming.

"Some bloody woman with a gun just stole my car!" An old man approached Sam rage in his face. Sam held up his hands as a crowd gathered.

"I'm a police officer," he lied, "She is Melanie Chambers and she is wanted for murder." There were gasps from the crowd.

"Which way is she headed?"

"Towards the falls, the road there leads you to either Leyburn eastwards or West to Hawes and right across the Pennines.

Sam took out his phone and called Christos. He gave him the details and then spoke to the gathered crowd.

"I need a vehicle just to get me to the falls," Sam pleaded. A young man spoke up,

"I'll take you." He turned with pride to a beaten-up old Ford Fiesta with a dent on the front and a sticker on the back that said "Farmers do it in the field." Sam looked quizzically at it, then got in the passenger seat. The young boy revved up the car and wheel span out of the farmyard. He raced skilfully through the narrow lanes and it wasn't long before he saw another ahead.

"That's her, that's grandad's car!" Sam held on tight as the boy increased his speed to what Sam thought was dangerous. He was close to the car in front.

"Slow down, I want her alive" Sam placed a warning hand on the boy's arm.

"Sorry," he braked and the car fell back some twenty yards.

"There's a junction ahead, almost opposite the falls." The boy spoke with some excitement.

SIXTY

In the car ahead, Melanie made a split-second decision; she spun the wheel to the left, skidded out of the junction and headed towards Hawes. A hundred yards in front, a black transit skidded to a halt and blocked the road.

"Shit!" Melanie shouted to no one but herself. She braked heavily, put the car in reverse, and spun the car around. Heading back the way she came, she could see another transit heading her way.

"Shit, shit shit!" There was a left turn ahead that led down to the Aysgarth Falls. She spun the wheel and skidded around the corner almost colliding with the young boy racer who was driving Sam in pursuit along the main road. The boy slammed on his brakes and stopped inches before the rear end of Melanie's car caught him. She revved up her engine and sped off down the lane towards the River Ure. The young boy racer looked at Sam who nodded encouragement, and he set off in pursuit of Melanie. It was early morning and there was no traffic to slow them down. Melanie pushed her car as fast as she dared on the unfamiliar road. She could see the other car in her mirror following her.

"Sam, just let me go!" she screamed. As she looked in her mirror to gauge the distance of the chasing car she failed to spot a sharp left-hand turn that led to a small single-track bridge over the river. When she re-focused on the road ahead, it was too late. She slammed on the brakes. The car skidded on the damp early morning tarmac and smashed into the safety railings on the bridge, wedging itself across the road. Melanie Chambers was thrown around the front seat like a rag doll. She had failed to put on her seat belt. Her head smashed against the side window and then was thrown back the other way, taking her body with her. Her legs stuck under the steering column for a moment before the momentum pulled her back the other way and she again struck her head against the window. This time it cracked. She screamed in agony as her bones creaked and remonstrated with her brain. Eventually, she was still, blood oozing from her ear and nose. Pain seared up her bruised legs and her shoulders screamed with tension. Steam rose from the crumpled bonnet of the car that was wedged up against the side of the bridge.

The screech of brakes and the sound of a car door opening roused her. She turned around to look and pain ripped through her neck.

"Shit, that hurts!" She scrambled to retrieve the Glock that had fallen into the footwell and then pushed the driver's door open. She almost fell out. Pain coursing through her body she ducked down behind the car. It acted as a barrier between her and Sam who stood behind the passenger door of the Ford Fiesta some twenty metres away, gun in hand.

"Mel, stop now, please. It's all over." Sam pleaded as he called out to her. The wind gusted and he shivered.

"I'll kill you, Sam, if you try to follow me. Stay there." She fired a warning shot over his head. Sam ducked down behind the car door. Melanie took her chance and hobbled across the bridge, her legs screaming in pain. At the far side of the bridge, she scrambled down to the riverbank to try to take cover in the woodland that ran beside the river. She slipped and nearly lost her footing. Above her, she heard Sam's footsteps running across the bridge. She turned and took a wild shot. Sam fell to the ground and used the low wall of the bridge as cover.

"Mel, it's dangerous, come back." Another shot rang out and ricocheted off the stone wall.

"Sod this! I've tried to be reasonable." Sam muttered. He slowly rose and put his head above the low wall. He saw Melanie scrambling along the edge of the river, darting in and out of the cover of the trees. He raised his pistol aimed as best he could, he was no marksman, and squeezed the trigger. The recoil surprised him and he nearly dropped the gun. The report of the pistol rang out.

Below on the river edge, Melanie heard the shot, it cracked a branch somewhere above her head. A red mist came down, ridding her of all sense and reason. *How dare he?*

She turned back to face the bridge and with the arrogance of one who believed that she had the right to kill others, fired back at Sam with a rapid string of shots that ricocheted around Sam, who ducked down rapidly. For a moment, there was silence. Sam raised his head. From some distance away, he heard a shout.

"Police. Freeze. Melanie Chambers, stop. Police." He saw her raise the gun one more time before a single shot rang out. Melanie was flung backwards, the top of her head disappearing in a cloud of red mist and brain matter. Her body hit the damp grass and rolled forward into the river. Sam watched as the swollen River Ure carried what used to be Melanie Chambers down its course, battering her body against the rocks.

SIXTY-ONE

Johnny Saint opened his eyes to see his two friends staring down at him. He was lying in bed in a private ward of the Darlington Memorial Hospital.

"Welcome back, my friend. I thought we'd lost you." There was real emotion in Sam's voice. Sally bent forward to kiss his forehead.

"What happened? The last I recall was Robert Frost pointing a gun at me." Johnny looked tired and in some pain.

"Well, apparently it's a miracle you're alive." Sam's broad smile told Johnny how much he cared. "It seems that you either moved out of the way a millisecond before he took his shot or…" His wife interrupted him.

"An angel pushed you!" She laughed as she spoke. Johnny looked at her for a moment wondering if she were serious. When he saw the glint in her eyes, he knew.

"How long have I been here?" Johnny tried to sit up, but the pain was acute.

"Sit still," said Sam. "Lucky for you, the bullet just went through muscle and missed all organs and main arteries. The chances of that are infinitesimal according to the doctors. Two days, you've been unconscious for two days."

"Lucky eh?" Johnny smiled a twinkle in his eyes. "What happened to Melanie and Robert?"

"Melanie is dead. She tried to escape, opened fire on police officers and was shot." Sadness flooded across Johnny's face. The death of another human always caused him grief, even if that person was trying to kill him.

"And Robert Frost?"

"He is on the run. He has disappeared. Now we have his laptop

Mark Savage used it legally to arrest all the others." Sam spoke with some pride.

"All but one." Sally corrected. "One woman, Nadir Safar, the Middle Eastern woman we saw on the video footage." There is no record of anyone with that name. She is a ghost. Whoever, she is, she too has vanished without trace."

"The Six is finished, it's over. We can all go back to peaceful life." Sam took his friend's hand and held it tight. "Mark Savage used his influence on the police and press. Apparently, you died at the scene. Therefore, if Frost escapes, he won't come looking for you. It's over." Sam was genuinely relieved.

"I am so glad you came back into my life Johnny. You have been a real blessing. As soon as you're up and about, your job will be waiting. You've got a glamping site to run and a shop to rebuild!"

"For a moment I thought you were being kind to me." They laughed, but Johnny winced as the stitches in his side pulled.

"Johnny?" said Sally hesitantly, "seeing as you're not dead, does that mean you are Saint John?"

"Yeah, old friend, Is Jesus coming back soon, coz that was a close shave?" Sam joined in.

Johnny looked at them both, shifting his gaze from one to the other, unsure of how to take their questions. He chose to deflect them.

"Sam, do I recall you saying you believed in God? Remember, when we were all up in the apartment and Frost had us a gunpoint? I am sure you said you believed in God. What about you Sal?" He turned to her, "Are you a believer too?" *If they can be mischievous, then I can too.* Sam flustered and Sally fidgeted, a flush of colour ran up her face.

"well… um… maybe?" Sam seemed to squirm, not knowing exactly what to say. He wanted to believe but didn't know what Sally thought. If he was going to believe, he wanted Sally by his side too.

"You'd better hurry up and decide," said Johnny, "If Jesus comes back, you might miss your chance?" There was a twinkle in his eye; he could see their discomfort. He began to laugh and they laughed along too.

"Maybe soon, just a bit more proof." Sam stood up. "Come on Sally, let's leave this man to get some rest."

SIXTY-TWO

The national and international news programmes were just about back to normal after the sensational discovery of a global terrorist organisation that had been exposed and dismantled through the cooperation of Interpol and various national security agencies. The biggest headline was that it was not religious but based on hedonistic, atheist principles. The majority of broadcasters could not understand how rational atheists and educated people would behave in such a way. There had been public television debates and investigations into the lives of the rich and famous who had been arrested as part of the operation to expose and close down The Six and its cover charity, Digamma.

The evidence of Robert Frost's laptop had been more than sufficient to convict every member of Digamma of conspiracy to commit terrorist acts. It also contained a great deal about the prominent UK celebrities who were the UK trustees of Digamma. Enough to discredit them socially as well as criminally. The media had a field day.

Religious commentators talked of sin and the impact it had on a broken humanity that needed a saviour, such as Jesus. Some spoke of Satan's influence, others that this was a sign of the apocalypse. They were mainly rejected by the mainstream media and given very little airtime in the wake of The Six's demise.

"*Two of the thirty-six members of Digamma, or The Six are still at large,*" the newscaster was saying as Sam and Sally watched the TV in their lounge. "*Robert Frost, a former aide to the Prime Minister and an unknown female going by the alias of Nadir Safir. It is thought they may be in hiding somewhere in the Middle East...*" Sam flicked off the TV with the remote and stood up. "Anyone else for another drink?"

It was Christmas Day; everyone who Sam dearly loved was with him. Sally, had just entered the room. He looked at her and smiled, as he always did. Ian and Kelly sat on the sofa. She was curled up like a kitten with her head in Ian's lap. Ian held up his beer and shook his head in response to Sam's question. Christos sat in the big wing-backed chair, by the fire, snoring. Maria and Thomas sat on the floor near the enormous Christmas tree, with its flickering lights and baubles. He was unwrapping yet another present. His mother Maria 'oohed' and 'aahed' at his excitement of another gift from Santa. Sally stood by the fire, having just finished clearing the table from a huge traditional Christmas dinner.

"I've done my bit, now it's your turn Sam Tucker. Get out there and take the rubbish out!" She kissed him on the lips and squeezed his bottom.

"Yes, Ma'am!" Sam grinned at his wife. Johnny Saint got up out of his chair,

"I'll help you, Sam." He made for the door quickly before Sally could stop him.

"Johnny, don't you do it all, I know you!" She pulled a face as if to say, *I know what you're up to.*

"No, I just need to talk to him. I'll make sure he takes the rubbish out." He winked at her.

In the cool of the kitchen, Johnny stood by the window, looking out over the yard as the afternoon winter sun slowly set. The barn with the shop and his apartment was covered in scaffolding and there were a couple of skips filled with burned wood, old doors and the detritus of a fire.

Johnny had spent several weeks reflecting and thinking about his future. Was it time to move on? Being shot and declared dead by the press, and the weeks of recovery had given him plenty of time to mull it all over. Still, he was unclear. He had been praying it through, seeking the guidance of the God he loved; talking with Sam about the role he was being offered as a site manager for the Glamping site, as well as supporting Ian. It was only last night that he was sure of his future. He felt strong again, refreshed as if he had gained several years back. The familiar voice in his mind had spoken clearly to him. *Sam still needs you here.*

"I've decided to take you up on the offer. I'd like to stay. If you'll have me."

"Of course I'll bloody have you." Sam stepped over to him, shook his hand and then moved in for a strong, long, man hug. Sam stepped back, looked his friend in the eye, and said.

"Right, now take that rubbish out." Johnny almost fell for it and went to pick up the black sack full of the remains of a busy Christmas Day.

"Hey," he paused realising his error, "that's not in my contract!"

Back in the lounge about twenty minutes later, Sam called his friends to order.

"Someone wake up Christos, please. His snoring is upsetting the dog." The room erupted into laughter and Ronnie barked happily. Christos jumped at the sound.

"What? Where?" his sleepy voice was still gruff and loud.

"Listen, everyone. I'm not one for speeches…"

"Thank God!" said Ian and again the room filled with laughter.

"Seriously, I just want to say thank you. It has been a strange, dangerous and enlightening six months. I am thankful we are all alive…"

"Hear, hear," said Johnny raising a glass of red wine. Everyone smiled and echoed his statement, raising their glasses.

"This arrived about three weeks ago." He held up an A4 envelope addressed to him, with the logo of a DNA company on the front.

The room went very still. Everyone just stared at the envelope. "It's the DNA test results that Christos sent off. The samples that Johnny gave us."

"Well open it then!" Christos boomed, his Greek accent seemingly more pronounced.

Sam turned to Johnny, who sat on the sofa facing the open fire. Johnny held his gaze. His eyes filled with love for his friend. He spoke quietly.

"There will be no going back, Sam. Are you ready for it? Is Sally ready for it?" Sam turned to his wife who looked nervously at her husband.

"If you are the apostle, then I can believe. So will Sally." She nodded her agreement.

But if I am not?" said Johnny solemnly, "will you reject God, because I am not an apostle? Will you reject it based on one DNA test? Faith is about trust." He looked Sam in the eyes.

"When Jesus spoke to Thomas after the resurrection, Thomas believed because he had seen Jesus. However, Jesus says to him, *Because you have seen me, you have believed; blessed are those who have not seen and yet have believed.* If you wait for one hundred per cent proof, you will be waiting forever. You have to take a step of faith. Only then will it become truly real."

"What do you mean?" Sally said questioningly, "real."

Johnny looked at her lovingly, smiled and spoke with gentle authority, as one who had experienced many things in his life. "I look at non-believers, agnostics and atheists and ask myself the question, 'Why is it they cannot see the truth that God is real and Jesus died for them?' but I also know that non-believers look at me and all believers and ask a similar question. 'Why do believers still believe in a mysterious superpower, even today in our world of technology, science and advancement, when humans are the masters of all they can see?'"

Sally smiled and nodded. "Truth is easy to see when you live in it every day."

"Yes, that's true, but there is so much more than just adhering to a set of principles or virtues. Genuine faith in Jesus is relational. Jesus loves you more than you can imagine and desires your love in return. That's why he died and rose again."

"So why did he allow Frost, Melanie and all the others to go around murdering, destroying stuff and behaving in the way they did? Why not just stop them?" Ian was sitting forward in his chair keen to engage with the growing debate.

Johnny was beginning to enjoy himself; he sipped his wine, placed it back on the coffee table and leaned forward.

"Does a loving and good parent wrap their children up in cotton wool and stop them from doing anything? Controlling their every movement? Or do they teach them right from wrong, show them how to live and ultimately let them go, even if they choose a life that the parent doesn't like. They still love them, don't they?"

"Freewill," said Maria, "We all have a choice; God is not a dictator but a loving father." Sally could see this going on all evening, so she stepped in.

"Hey, it's Christmas Day, not a theological discussion group. That was getting heavy. Let's play charades!" There was laughter all around.

"I'm not going anywhere for a while, so if you want to talk some more, just ask me!" Johnny beamed as he spoke. He knew in his heart that things were changing for this group of friends. They were on a journey.

"There's just one more thing," he said looking at Sam. "What are you going to do with that envelope?" Sam held the envelope up; he had forgotten all about it as the discussion unfolded.

"I'm not sure I'm ready to know yet. I have a few more questions." With that, he tossed the envelope into the open fire where it burned rapidly, the paper curling as the flames took hold. Everyone stared wide-eyed.

Sally stepped over to her husband and whispered in his ear, "When you're ready I'll be ready too." She kissed his cheek. He smiled at her, he always did.

Later that evening, as he sat nursing a cup of tea in the kitchen, Johnny held a gift in his hand. It felt like a book. It was wrapped in brown parcel paper as opposed to Christmas gift wrap. Sally insisted everything be recyclable. He undid the paper and slipped out the book. Flipping it over so he could see the cover, he read it and smiled. *"I am John" by Samuel E. Tucker.*

"I thought you could tell me if I am on the right lines. Have I got it all right? I mean, you were there, right?" The smirk on Sam's face filled Johnny with joy.

SIXTY-THREE

Robert Frost reclined on a sun lounger on the deck of a large yacht anchored in the Gulf of Arabia off the coast of Dubai. He wore swimming trunks and nothing else. It was a warm sunny Christmas Day. He sat up removed his sunglasses and looked around the deck.

"Nadir? Where are you?" He called out. His voice carried the same authority that had enthralled and aroused Melanie Chambers. Nadir Safir emerged from the stateroom of the yacht carrying two glasses of cold champagne. She wore a very small black bikini that revealed more than it hid. Her olive skin and loose black hair blowing gently in the sea breeze made her look like an exotic model. *A goddess*, thought Robert, ironically. He looked at her closely; the past few weeks with Nadir had been totally captivating. She was supreme in every way. She was intelligent, stylish, committed to the Atomist cause and not least, she was excellent between the sheets. All thoughts of Melanie had evaporated the moment he had met Nadir. He had toasted her life when the news reported her death and that of Johnny Saint, but that was it. Nadir was in a different league. When they weren't having sex, they planned the regeneration of The Six under a new name and new structure. Their mission would not die. He smiled as she approached him. She responded. She placed the champagne down on the table.

"I thought you might like another glass." She bent down and kissed him, rubbing her hand over his chest. He could feel himself becoming aroused, his base instincts kicking in. She stood back undid her bikini top and let it fall to the deck beside the lounger. Putting her thumbs inside her bikini bottoms, she lowered them and stepped out of them, tossing them aside.

"Would you like me to massage you? " She picked up some sun oil and waved it in her hands. Frost was mesmerised.

"Of course you would my darling," she whispered not giving him a choice. She leaned forward and tugged his shorts off, throwing them aside.

"Turn over and I will start with your back." Frost eagerly turned over and lay front down on the lounger. Nadir eased herself onto his back and sat astride his buttocks. She leaned forward and kissed him on the head.

"Just relax; you'll soon be in heaven!" He was about to make a comment about not believing in it when Nadir swiftly grabbed her bikini top and skilfully wrapped it around his neck, pulling it tight. Frost began to choke, to scramble and try and move, but she clamped him with her thighs and continued to pull on the bikini. He tried to speak but couldn't. His arms flailing, trying to catch Nadir and push her away. She was strong and practised in the art of subduing men.

"Let me say it for you Robert. I know what you want to say. 'Why?' You want to know why you will die today." Her accent became stronger as she concentrated on keeping the pressure on his neck. "You are weak, controlled by your groin. You killed the wrong man; Johnny Saint was no apostle. You failed in every task you attempted, and you are not worthy to be one of The Six. If we are to rise again, I will lead us. You think you know me, Robert, because I let you use my body. No, I used you."

Roberts's eyes were bulging, he was fading fast, his awareness slipping away, and the light in his eyes was growing dim. Before the darkness overtook him, he heard his killer speak one last time.

"In your weakness, your rush to take my body for your pleasure, you gave me everything. Do you remember? You were high on cocaine and drunk with alcohol. Your money, property, and investments are all mine, every single million." She paused so he could assimilate this final piece of knowledge. "So weak, Robert, so weak. You will die a pauper, alone at sea, no one will ever know. Shark food."

Nadir Safir slipped on her bikini and tied up the limp cadaver that had been Robert Frost. She then tied one of the weights from the Yacht's gymnasium to his feet, dragged him to the back of the deck to the dingy platform and pushed him overboard. She watched as the body slowly sank beneath the gentle waters of the Gulf.

Turning back to the wheelhouse, she powered up the yacht and headed back towards Dubai.

ABOUT THE AUTHOR

Jez Taylor

Jez Taylor is a retired secondary school teacher living in Sussex. This is his fourth novel but the first attempt at a thriller. He is married with two adult children. He is an active member of his local Baptist church. He enjoys playing golf and is a keen Fulham fan.

BOOKS BY THIS AUTHOR

On This Rock

2000 yrs. ago the nation of Israel was under the oppressive rule of the Romans. A young boy, Simon, grew up hearing the stories of freedom; stories of how God would send his Messiah to free Israel from all her enemies. He knew the prophecies; he dreamed the dreams of freedom. As a young married man, he lived to provide for his family; his dreams of freedom shattered by the power of Rome. That is until he meets a wandering Rabbi called Yeshua. His life gets turned upside down. Could this man be God's chosen Messiah? Simon finds himself on a journey of discovery which takes him from being a small time fisherman to becoming the leader of a band of twelve revolutionaries who are set to change the world.

I Will Build My Church

Jesus has ascended to heaven and the fledgling Church is led by Peter, who discovers that with the power of the Holy Spirit, he can see God's kingdom grow. Encountering many obstacles such as persecution and dissension from within his community, he sees the Church flourish from being a small sect to a major influence in the Roman world. Essentially a family man, Peter has to make difficult choices to ensure he fulfils his duty to Jesus and his family.

I Don't Care Who Started It

Jack Turner has seen it all in his life as a secondary school teacher. Starting as a humble RE teacher in a large Sussex school, he rose to become an assistant head and school leader. This book is a series of snapshots that recall significant moments, heart-warming times, steep learning curves, frustrations, mistakes and much more. Anyone who has been a teacher or has worked in a school will resonate with Jack's story, will laugh and cry, and share in his rollercoaster life at the chalk face.

SAINTS AND SINNERS

Saints and Sinners follows the adventures of Sam and Sally Tucker as they battle the mysterious atheistic terror group "The Six", whose aim is to destroy faith and religion in favour of a hedonistic, elitist society. As they do so they become more aware of spritual elements of life and how important they are to their own wellbeing and that of others too. The Six must be stopped before they damage the world beyond repair.

Book One-I Am John

Whilst researching his book, lottery winner Sam Tucker and his wife Sally become embroiled in the hunt for a mysterious religious figure, a man called John. Can they find him before the atheistic terrorist group 'The Six' captures him? 'The Six' believe his death to be vital in their plan to undermine all religious belief and create a hedonistic, elitist world where the pleasures of the senses rule over the rights of the poor. Can Sam and Sally stop 'The Six' and in doing so protect the life of an innocent man? What they uncover, if true, would turn the world upside down.
From Sussex to Jerusalem via the Greek Islands, the story twists and turns until its thrilling climax in the heart of the Yorkshire Dales.

Book Two-Ferry To Maddalena

Sam and Sally are on the trail of the new leader of The Six and uncover a plot that will bring chaos to central London, cause irreparable damage to the relationship between the world faiths and potentially lead to a global religious war.

The book is not yet complete but will hopefully be by the end of 2024

Book Three- As Yet Untitled

No plot yet, book two needs to be finished first.

Printed in Great Britain
by Amazon